Also by Neil Claremon

East by Southwest *(poems)* 1970

West of the American Dream *(poems)* 1973

BORDERLAND

NEIL CLAREMON

BORDERLAND

A NOVEL

ALFRED A. KNOPF · NEW YORK · 1975

THIS IS A BORZOI BOOK

PUBLISHED BY ALFRED A. KNOPF, INC.

Copyright © 1975 by Neil Claremon

All rights reserved under International and Pan-American Copyright

Conventions. Published in the United States by Alfred A. Knopf, Inc.,

New York, and simultaneously in Canada by Random House of Canada

Limited, Toronto. Distributed by Random House, Inc., New York.

Library of Congress Cataloging in Publication Data

Claremon, Neil. Borderland. I. Title.

PZ4.C5894B03 [PS3553.L25] 813'.5'4 74-21331

ISBN 0-394-49619-1

Manufactured in the United States of America

First Edition

This book is for my mother and father.

A certain ability to fly produces a change of environment, or behaviour towards environment, which favours an accumulation of the same ability. . . .

Erwin Schrödinger: *Mind and Matter*

BORDERLAND

"A man should not speak of such times and the dangers that are there."

"Nonetheless, I remember how it was with you when it seemed at its worst."

"Will you speak of what you should not have seen, so the words can live in the walls like enemies? It was unusual that you were with me—you could speak of how this came to be. That could be counted above the silence."

"A man can speak of birth if he was there."

"There are words that are wrong in your mouth and it is still strange among my people that you found me."

"That's because they feel the birth was sorcery, and still speak about it with disapproving wonder. Yet it was possible because of those times that came before."

"*Then as any man would tell of a battle he has fought, tell how you came to the knowledge of those days. This would make it easier for us to live together here, for there are many around us who live in the darkness inside. You can choose the words so they will not fall into that world of fear.*"

"*I should make all I remember very real to them so they will accept me again.*"

"*I cannot stop you from saying what you want to, but there is a trust between us, and wasn't I most yours at that hour when death was most near? That time of night when the will is strongest or weakest is the still point between dusk and dawn, and even the creatures of the desert fear the moment when it comes.*"

"*But that time when the night holds us in its sway is not always to be feared, and I wonder: Would you make love with me then?*"

"*No. We enter that region on our prayers.*"

Two

On the day near the end of her eighth month when she suddenly vanished, not telling anyone where she was going, the women were intent on the evening's beef and tortillas and on their wood-burning stoves as I kept asking if they had seen her, and they threw up their hands, saying: *"The first house is the house of gloom and inside there is only darkness."*

I'd heard this expression before—a proverb about our mystifying lot on earth—which excused almost everything that went on. Most things were done under the shadow of this attitude but matter-of-factly, and as the custom was for women to go off alone when the time came, I became concerned about her.

Near the hacienda was a small riverbed, or arroyo, which

was her favorite spot to retreat to. It was just like her to leave without speaking to me, and I went east along the arroyo, thinking that darkness always comes from the east, and walked through a surreal latticework of thorn branches growing from the rocky desert crevices and trees which became sentinels against a darkening sky. I could barely distinguish the shapes and forms around me, and for quite some time I felt I was so near that I could touch her.

When I entered her hastily thrown-together shelter, she lay on her side, apparently sleeping, her arm held on the full mound of her belly. The brown earth in the dark mingled with her clay-brown skin, blurring all contours. The earth was soft and loose as sand, and she had made it this way, hoeing it with her bare feet. She was surrounded by dry clumps of weeds and darkness, and her hair, tucked to one side, rested like linen folded between her and the sand.

I knelt by the entrance and could not think of anything to say.

"You should not have followed me," she said suddenly.

"I didn't know where you were."

"How did you find me? You don't belong here, please," she continued, still facing away from me.

"What are you doing here alone?" I asked, trying gently to scold her.

"Go away before your white cock drops off and you lose your self."

I was sure she was delirious, although she certainly recognized me.

"How could you find me?" she asked.

"A foxfire," I said.

"You are loco. Why don't you go back and wait for me?"

"Let me hold you first," I said with the intention of trying to soothe her. I wasn't crazy, in fact. She had built her enclosure in a thicket of mesquite on a knoll in the bend of the arroyo, and I wouldn't have seen it except for that luminescent glow on dead branches, which I could not pass by.

"It is my time to be alone," she said, and screamed *Aie! Aie!* as I moved toward her. It seemed inhuman for her to wish to be alone.

"It's too soon, unless it is a false labor," I said. There was another thought I could not air; that she was about to lose this child, for she had miscarried before. There was no point in going for a doctor since one could not arrive in time to be of any use. I had to see what use I might be.

"Are you gone?" she cried out without raising her head from the sand.

I didn't know what to do; I saw she had brought her plants, which meant she had prepared herself to be alone here. In an open kerchief beside her were a narcotic mushroom, a common soap from the yucca, and a part of the barrel cactus. By my feet were several stalks from a rare *gomilla* plant she believed would stop hemorrhaging. I didn't know what else fit into her hasty arrangement of zacatón fibers woven across the thorny mesquite branches; and, entangled in that foliage we kept our silence like strangers.

Her breathing was shallow, almost restful, and it was my own that pulsed.

She drew her knees under her belly, assuming a foetal position, and I saw that the amniotic sac had broken, coating her thighs like some misaimed ejaculation. This was one signal of impending birth, but she lived in communal surroundings and must have known it sometimes happens weeks before.

I watched the rising moonlight playing on her wet skin.

She stretched out on her back, now in the grip of a mild contraction that hardly made her body shudder, merely forcing her to hold her breath. She seemed unconcerned by this event, too much so.

"Should I get someone from the ranch?" I suggested.

"Stay with me if you must. I may be somewhere else but I will be here until you leave." Her eyes turned to me in a way reminiscent of our passion for each other, but her words made no sense. She was more like a woman stricken by deep mourning than by pain, and I decided to wait. I couldn't read her mind and she was in some danger.

"Is the baby coming?" I asked.

"You must go before then, for if you stay you will never be the same."

"I will be all right," I said confidently. "Even if the baby does not come now, we will be all right."

There was a strong smell of urine in the air which moved as freely as the moonlight through the loosely woven zacatón. Her hand clutched at the soft earth, and her wide-eyed expression moved somewhere between pain and pleasure. Then came the next contraction, once again a short, weak spasm that she barely responded to. She was not exerting any effort to help her body, but was receding into a distant, trancelike state. A glazed look came over her features, a torpor which drained the gleam of her black eyes.

"Please tell me what is happening," I pleaded.

Silence.

Her dress was hiked up to the swollen breasts, revealing the hugely distended belly and navel. It frightened me: loving her had its alluring, primitive side, and I was now thrust into the other face of our lovemaking, and as she warned, a veil was falling between us. She had done this before, this leaving; and while I was straining to comfort her, or to aid her, everything in my rational being told me that she needed help and that I shouldn't wait for morning. Yet, since I'd crossed the border I'd seen what was possible, that there was more than we usually expect from one another, and I began to listen for the voice that would tell me what she would have done if I were lying there.

Three

It seems that we search all around to find what is inside that will preserve us. When I came here I was looking for the underground basin where the river might settle back on itself after coming out of the mountains. I had aerial maps and was trying to trace the invisible flow beneath the high plain, to check the feasibility of irrigation. The terrain itself made my task nearly impossible, and what I found first was the beginning of my unordinary fatherhood.

I felt that the countryside had a life of its own. The wind-swept foothills rolled beneath the desert floor and the backbone of mountains. The mountains moved with the play of sunlight and the sweep of the clouds, moved to their own mysterious heartbeat as protectors of the hills which fell under their shadow, turning into grasslands knotted with cactus and rock. I found it a country of mixtures, of silences, and sudden shifts of mood.

It was possible to survey fifty miles in any direction, and yet it would take hours to locate a single spot marked on the map. But the spareness and the vastness made me feel worth more, more distinguished, just as coming upon one cow alone on a hillside made it worth more at that moment than a whole herd. So there was a curious frustration in continually getting lost and in not being able to distinguish one landmark from another. I was constantly on the lookout for the desert's wildlife and kept by my side a camera with a telephoto lens. I had no desire to hunt but being alert to any movement on the terrain helped pass the time I spent driving.

On a ridge that afforded a good overview of the many arroyos coming out of the mountains, I was scanning the land and recording it—using the camera's viewfinder to get a closer impression—when I noticed flocks of birds. There were several distinct groupings over a single hill. I saw crows, then doves, then ravens, and I could not imagine what would bring them all together in a single place. Over the hill they broke their flight pattern and began swirling around. Some landed, and some only circled and resumed their flight. It was odd behavior and I decided to find out what was causing it.

As a high cloud, a single one, passed between me and the September sun, the light changed, and since it was less intense I could see more clearly. That's when I first saw her, a woman standing on the top of the hill, the birds circling around her. I couldn't tell what she was doing, but it seemed that she was attracting the birds. When she moved the birds came closer. Such cause and effect was tantalizing and I became more intent on reaching the hill.

Finally, instead of being near her at once, I wound up on a rocky terrace that came up above her. She was among the trees and as she moved between them the cacophony of the birds increased and they skittered along the plane of the sky, creating an invisible web in the air. I kept catching sight of her long sacklike dress flowing through the branches; the wind caught it and twisted it around her body at the moment I called out to her. She abruptly faced the top of the hill, not seeing me right away. Then she began to come toward me, hesitating as if she were trying to decide what kind of animal I was. She was no longer a girl, I saw, and hadn't the fine features or lithe body of a young woman. Her black hair and dark skin had a pleasant warmth, but I wouldn't have called her pretty. Though quite tall, her body seemed stocky, and her walk as she came closer was more than anything else a shuffle. It was quite sensual and I suppose I stared too hard at the outline of her large breasts loose against the cloth.

"What would you want?" she asked in a throaty, resonant voice.

"I was watching the birds," I said.

"What for?"

"I thought it was strange, that's all."

"Are you lost?"

"No."

"Then what are you doing here? If I want to see a white man, I will go into town. And when I want to be alone, I come down to the hills where there is nobody wandering around."

We were speaking in her mixture of Spanish and Piman, which I could get by in since I had done research among the Papagos on their reservation south of Tucson. But she now said something which I could not quite understand. I asked her to repeat it slowly. She laughed and her face broadened, taking on a more oval shape, a smile with cheekbones made pronounced by her small nose and high forehead. She said, "For what I am doing, I did not need a scarecrow." It wasn't the kind of remark to make me feel sure of myself.

"What are you doing here?" I asked, hoping to reach a firmer base.

"I may show you," she said, "but first I wonder if you have water in your canteen." She had finally given me a chance to move toward her, which I did while unstrapping the canteen. As she took it I noticed that her hands were all scratched. She turned around and proceeded to drink nearly the entire contents.

"What were you doing before?" I asked.

"I am a woman who has to take care of herself," she said, which failed to explain what she was doing with the birds.

She started toward the trees while telling me that the

spring she'd expected to find was dry, and I followed her among the trees, which were some common species. As we approached one with small leaves, thorns, and shiny branches, most of the birds darted to the next, but three flapped their wings as if to fly, yet remained stuck in a clear substance, some variety of resin that the tree produced in abundance at this time of year. Two large doves and a crow were caught in this resin, and I understood that she was trapping them.

The crow kept screaming at the top of its lungs, as she reached through the thorns to the doves and swiftly silenced them. The crow was another matter, and she asked me to help her. As I held the branches back she managed to get close to the crow. Gently she calmed the bird by stroking its back feathers and nape of the neck with a small stick. Treating it like one might handle a parakeet, she freed its legs from the sap and with a shove nudged it into flight.

We went from tree to tree until she filled the basket she had strapped to her back. "What are you called?" I asked as we sat down for a rest, before leaving.

"Can you say *Tsari?*" she asked.

"Tsari," I said.

"That's what I am called," she retorted.

"You live in the mountains?" I continued, assuming she was one of the Opatas who still lived at an old mountain rancheria which had become a village.

"I live in that place where a great cloud was seen in the sky. The cloud, we say, was the reflection of our mountains. At one time old people came together there and burned incense and danced, and said: 'Make the earth nourish and sustain us; invoke and remember us.' Then they built our rancheria." She looked toward the mountains, saying, "It is not such an easy thing to live there; it is all changed."

"You might move down with the Mexicans," I said, as a gesture of sympathy.

"Would you leave your home?"

"I don't know," I said, wishing to retract my suggestion, for I had no such place. I was one of those drifting, making my way through the Southwest, taking whatever job was offered at the moment. I wanted to change the subject and asked: "What will you do with the birds?" expecting an invitation to share them.

"Are you hungry?" she asked.

"I am," I said, "and thirsty." Then I tried a pun in her language revolving around the word hungry for food and hungry for loving. I wasn't sure that she had heard it, but her reply was, "It is best to fill one's belly." I was taken aback by the perfection of her answer and wasn't sure that she had not inadvertently proposed something.

We freed a last few birds as the light began to fade behind the mountains, and I accepted her invitation to eat, suggesting that we go back to the village in my jeep. She agreed and I pointed out where I had left it.

As we began to leave the clump of trees and I offered to carry her basket, I began to feel uneasy. There were no other birds around anywhere, and I had no idea how she had attracted these in the first place. I asked her but my question was none too clear, because the ability to summon flocks of birds was truly inconceivable. She said she didn't know what I was talking about, and it became difficult for me to leave the hill without constantly looking back.

Four

A month's work in the hills proved a lonely but not thankless task. Tsari intrigued me, but it was never the right time to return to the village since Brito was impatient for results. He needed an estimate of the water supply on the ranch and he wanted to know where it was abundant enough for farming. After studying most of his land I had eliminated all but one area as a potential spot. It was a dry lake sitting on a formation suitable for holding water. I felt there would be some water below the surface, although there was a good chance it wouldn't be enough. Brito wanted to check it out immediately, but the truth was, I was unsure.

I had a knack for tracing water, or believed I did, because of a mystical disaffinity with it. If there was no water around I felt better. I had a specialist's trade and all the credentials to back up my peculiar talent. The science of finding water was much easier for me because of the intuitions I had learned to trust; and the fact was that none of my employers particularly cared how the water was found, just as long as I located it. Brito was the loosest person I had ever worked for, willing to discuss even the art of water-witchery and letting me work on my own timetable, believing that on certain days one's faculties reached heightened perceptions.

That morning, after a quick breakfast, we drove the cow trails that ran between the hills until we came to the large sandy bowl carved between the end of the mountain range and the mesa that seemed to come out of its belly and slide like a smooth lava-flow toward the town. The dry lake was over a mile long and we decided to walk to the middle of it. From what I could tell from the formations, the lake had not had surface water since the last flood period over fifty years ago. It was a drainage area nonetheless and only a time of drought like we were in could dry it completely.

Brito waddled through the deep sand. He was getting paunchy and the determination creasing his round, rather babyish face made him look comical. We both had trouble walking and the sand was too hot for us to remove our boots. I was looking toward the mountains when he tripped and his hat blew off, and in brief anger he appeared more menacing.

"You are thinking about something else, my friend," he said as he got up. "Perhaps that is why I fall, no?"

I decided to tell him about my meeting with Tsari, indicating that she had been quite friendly; at least I thought so after comparing her to the others at the village, who ignored me.

"I am surprised," he interrupted. "She does not often take up with men. Like me, I think she knows she will never marry, but my problem is that I like too many women." We both laughed about such a weakness. "She must like the look of you," he concluded.

"I hope so," I said, "because I want to see as much of her as I can." I hoped he would catch the hint that I'd like to get back to the village.

"I understand what you are thinking about," he said, "and perhaps you should go see her again while on an errand for me. Her father is brother to the headman and I want to send him a message. If you are to spend time with Tsari, it will be a wild card; and you could fit into my plans in a new way if you are accepted by her."

"If it means a few days there now," I said, "then I'm ready to go anytime."

"When you go I would like you to tell her father and his brother that we have plans to irrigate this basin by spring, and that there will be a life here for all of them."

"I can do that easy enough," I said.

"You know, the Opatas are the best farmers in this part of the world. Their feeling for plants is worth more than all the equipment I can buy. I would like their village to be down here."

"Moving the village sounds a bit selfish, I think."

"There is no farming in the mountains anymore, not since the dam. I think it is a law of some kind that people will live near what they do best, given the chance."

He made it sound so simple. He was a short, strutting, pudgy man with a wry smile, and it was this easy charm that made me question the way he laid his plans out.

"Are you sure it is best for them to move down here?" I asked, hoping for a specific reason.

"It is just something I know," he said. "Those of us from the mountains have our own reasoning."

I didn't think of him as one of the people of the mountains, since his ranch was the largest landholding in this area, and he seemed rather worldly. "I'd just like to keep her friendly," I said.

"You may if you go slowly," he said. "You were too anxious to come here and it almost cost you this job, yet since the water-management people I asked told me you would work for a year, I decided that you would be more committed than those with reputations so good they could only work for a month."

We sat down on one of the many logs of petrified wood and it seemed we were the only living beings left on this lunar landscape where the beach had no ocean and the driftwood was made of stone, and I thought about the proposition to help him at the village.

"I don't really want to say anything about water until I find it and check the salt and alkaline content," I said.

"Right now that's not what's worrying me," he began,

"and if you look carefully at the mesa you'll see why I came with you."

I looked up to a rock formation, shaped like an aircraft carrier, understanding that it was not a natural mesa but rather the slag heap of a mining operation. The odd shape set into the haze that faced us was not simply rocks, nor was the haze natural.

"That smelter," Brito said, "dumps its waste down the side, and as you know, they must use a water runoff which will eventually drain into this area. Copper smelting does not produce the best chemicals for plants and farmers. I am going to leave you here with the jeep to make your tests, and I will walk up to the old mountain and see just how the drainage works. We will meet in the morning."

"You've got a lonely trip ahead of you," I said, surprised he would want to go off alone.

"No," he said, "the night is a good friend."

The next morning, after I had finished collecting what I needed and had packed the jeep, there was no sign of Brito. The equipment I needed to make further analysis was at the ranch and I was impatient to get back. I tried napping, but I wasn't tired and was actually trying to make him appear by closing my eyes. I tried using the camera to scan the barren mesa feeling sure that I would see him. I forced myself to keep examining the landscape, watching for movement. The sun was too bright to allow me to focus well and if I saw what I thought was a person, I could never quite make out whether it was or it wasn't. Each shape or motion I saw on the side of the mesa became diffused in the bright shimmer of sunlight along the rocks. By noon the glare was overwhelming, and the wind came up, driving the hot particles of sand against the jeep. I could hear a scuttling or rattle like blowing paper or cans, and then a chanting from a chorus of wind, while the minutes crept by, the air charged with jamming presences as I thought about going after Brito. I imagined something had happened to him, and I felt very uncomfortable waiting, unsure of what to do. The dust and wind were deceptive and I kept thinking I heard his voice. I knew I was losing control when there seemed to be myriad bodies wavering off in the distance.

Then I remembered that Brito had not said we should meet back here in the morning. I started the jeep and the familiar sound of the engine dispelled my fears. I didn't understand what had made me so uneasy until I realized that there had to be plenty of water in the basin under me. It was my disaffinity again. I could smell that water waiting underground, and felt I had just received a gift.

Five

Her village was the center of life for those Indians in the mountains, and yet without having been shown where it was, I would not have been able to find it. It reminded me of the formless outskirts of a Mexican city, with each house blending into its own cluster of outbuildings and corrals. Each cluster had its own edges, but they, being made out of anything that was available—wood, adobe, tin, or thatch—blended into the next. Nothing looked modern or new, and the village collapsed upon itself, but the impression of decay was deceptive. It was larger than it looked and there was always another house after the village seemed to end, a stream of dwellings wandering off into the fall-colored woods. There were over four hundred people, and it surprised me that so many were able to support themselves.

The drive up went quickly because of what was on my mind. Brito had told me that a dam along our border sharply reduced the water supply to the village, making farming dependent entirely on seasonal rains, and that the drought was causing the younger men to seek work at the mine, while the government was doing everything it could to force the others from their retreat at the top of the *barranca*, so that they might be more easily looked after. The entrance to the village was a steep, narrow pass between the cliffs which gave access to the area at the timber line, and it was the most difficult part of the drive. I kept thinking about Brito's message promising water and farming, and about being invited to stay with Tsari, but I wasn't sure that they were compatible purposes.

She was at her father's house when I arrived and I explained why I had returned. She didn't seem pleased by my reason, but Silvera invited me to attend a meeting of their council. While I had a moment alone with Tsari, I told her how glad I was to see her again and that I had been thinking about her constantly. She refused to pay attention to me, and I was disconcerted, for I was telling the truth.

I went into a building much like all the others. Inside were three men. I could barely catch what they were talking about, for they were sitting by the rear wall. There seemed to be an angry tone to their conversation; I was asked to sit on a concrete block by the doorway, while my host joined the session. It was easy to tell which of the three men was Silvera's brother because the headman was also powerfully built, and had the same long, silver-streaked hair. I had been impressed by the remarkable look of health of everyone in the village, especially the older people. The headman had a definite command, an inner strength, and his brother's face indicated a similar nature.

"This man is gringo," the headman said, finally deigning to look at me.

"I must speak for this man," his brother said, "whether I know him or not, because he has come here for our benefit."

"We should not be generous with this man," the chief said. "We should not receive him. We should not treat him kindly."

I had a carefully prepared presentation to make with maps and charts, explaining that water was collecting in the underground basin at the edge of the mountains below the village and that even though it was not visible, it was there. It was not a social issue.

"Tell me why we should even listen to a gringo," the headman said while the two men in the middle conferred with each other. "Before we listen to anyone anymore, we should take back what is ours. There is plenty of time for talk, when there is plenty to drink."

I was beginning to see what was at stake in this discussion.

One man said, "When there is no trouble, it is bad to make a change. Whatever happens, if we change there is more danger."

The chief, I believed, was asking for some action against

the dam, and I didn't want to say any more, for I didn't understand exactly what I was getting into.

The silent man said, "We have the stones entrusted to us by our fathers, and still it is not clear what we should do."

"They must be passed on to our children," the chief said.

"They will not be passed on to anyone if the children leave and work in mines and in towns. The village must be moved to a better place," his brother answered.

"The village will not hold any power to keep us together if we move it," the chief replied. "We cannot leave this place."

I could see no resolution to their deadlock. Brito had sent me here to play both sides against the middle. I didn't like it, and I didn't know what would be best for the Indians, or how Brito could be so certain he was right.

"I would like to speak," I said, wanting to apologize.

"It is not your decision," the chief said. "We have not asked you to."

"I think this man brings us a fair offer from Brito. He has not said this but that is what his being here means," Tsari's father said.

"Brito's land would never be ours. The offer is not real. I think you should call your daughter," the chief concluded.

I had no idea why the woman had to be called but when her father returned with her, we all went outside and stood in front of the house. She had put on a bright purple blouse and a long blue skirt which touched the ground. These colors enhanced her appearance and this time I thought she was younger and more attractive.

The chief addressed her, "Is this man your friend?"

"Yes," she answered, almost defiantly, and I was pleasantly surprised that she had decided to claim me.

"Then he belongs to you," the chief said. "Nothing has been gained or lost by his coming, nothing will be gained or lost by his leaving."

"I understand," she said and looked to her father for approval.

"It is not our concern what you do with him," he said, smiling for the first time.

At first, I was relieved to be turned over to her care. I had come to do an errand for Brito, and the men were right in not listening to me, for I had nothing of my own to say to them. But when they turned me over to Tsari it was a polite slap in the face, for I was not yet a man to be considered and had to be turned over to a woman like a little boy. I had failed to pass through a fence but had no idea how to rearrange things.

We walked through the village and she was glad to show me around. We watched the children. If they were shabby, they were also alert and indifferent to the conditions around them. I watched them for a while, trying to figure out what game they played in the absence of toys and playgrounds. The girls and boys seemed to be acting in two separate groups, but as they kept laughing at each other from time to time, I had to conclude that they were playing together. One at a time, the girls would break away from the group and race off into the squares of corrals and houses. In a few minutes one of the boys would dash off in the same direction, cheered on by his companions. When he came back after a short time, the girls would be giggling and playing with their skirts, for they were enjoying themselves at their form of hide-and-seek.

Their enjoyment turned into a mockery of my own discomfort. I wanted to remain with Tsari, but my stated purpose was finished, and though I tried to explain that I had come to visit her, she said she had chores to do further up in the mountains that night.

Six

"I would like to talk about the village," I told Brito when I saw him the next morning, for I was still dismayed by the reception I got at the village.

"This is not the place to talk about it," he said, "but we will go to a more suitable one. I've been wondering about your reaction ever since you returned."

"I don't see what place has to do with it," I replied, for I was impatient to have an explanation. But Brito evaded my questions, and we left the Abulafia hacienda in his rebuilt army truck—a beaten-up vehicle with special torque and handling equipment working away beneath the old frame. We drove into the hills and it seemed that we were going nowhere in particular. As we curved in and out of the view of the mountains, I kept seeing black objects against the sky. They appeared to be buzzards but they held in formation, and this was indeed odd for birds that ride the wind currents. I watched them as if they were mirages, my mind on other things.

Brito turned off the road, and as we entered a branch of the arroyo, he said: "I didn't think you would react with such concern; most visitors would have believed the people were just cautious. I have to give you more credit than I expected, for it is not easy to tell the differences up there."

"You could have told me about the chief's hostile attitude toward strangers."

"I didn't realize you would care, so I never thought it was necessary. Any stranger would have been resented at this time, and will be for as long as the dam exists along the border and the river is diverted into the States. The Opatas hold both countries responsible and receive visitors grudgingly. And there are traditions which will make it difficult for you."

"I've been wondering about that too," I said.

"You will understand more when we get to the place we are going."

"Where's that?" I asked, for we were driving down the middle of the arroyo.

"My greenhouse," he said.

We arrived at a narrow canyon safely tucked away between the hills where rock walls formed a natural enclosure and a spring supplied an abundance of water. Here Brito had developed an extensive garden. I knew he liked plants, that they were his hobby, but I never expected a perfectly planned and concealed horticultural laboratory. "As a child I had a green thumb," he said, "and now you see how well my children are doing." I did, but I didn't know what to make of it.

"This little canyon," he continued, "it once belonged to a man named Tamayo, an Opata who raised goats and kept an herb garden, the best in all Sonora. He was already old when I knew him, a survivor of the Yaqui wars. All he wanted was peace and seclusion, and because the ranch has always been neutral ground he finally got his freedom. It was he who gave me the idea for this place."

"This is no small undertaking," I said, but could not figure out why there were no crops, houseplants, or flowers.

"Two years' work," he said. "And here I have plants from all over Mexico and Central America. Some are herbs, and some you might call drugs. It does not matter. They are all medicines."

"Are they for the mind or for the body?" I asked, somewhat suspicious.

"What is the difference? You make a distinction that has no meaning for me. When I grew up I witnessed some remarkable performances. Those who heal with plants are now considered dangerous, but in my youth I became interested in such skills, only to find out I didn't have them. Yet here I have accumulated the most famous of the native remedies. You may think it is a useless task, but as the medicine of the doctors reaches its limit and they find there are ailments they cannot cure by their methods, then people will again look into the art of the old healers."

"And Tamayo was such a healer?"

"A healer of animals. He was very welcome here at the ranch and it was through him that my father met my mother. He believed that much sickness was only an imbalance of the body caused by the mind and the diet. He used plants such as those around us to make his cures. I could have learned what to use from him, but it is not simply a matter of medicines. It was his will-powers and knowledge of the illnesses' effect on the body that made him so remarkable. He had the gift to make even a goat or a cow the desire to heal itself. This is the great healing power that cannot be learned. It develops in a tradition the doctors still ignore, and they often fail by ignoring the will of the patient altogether. Don't we depend on being in tune with the inner forces as well as the outer ones? You will not believe that Tamayo lived well past one hundred."

"If you don't have such powers, how can you be certain about them? It makes me wonder about Tsari and the birds again."

"I believe she plays around with such knowledge as Tamayo had, for that is her temperament, but I am not sure she will become a *curandera*."

"How do you know she does?" I asked.

"I don't really know, and I come here to forget my problems at the ranch and with the village. It is the only place

I can be without feeling that all is hopeless, as if the spirit of the old man still pervades this canyon," he continued as he bent down to touch a small plant that grew a delicate fur. He stroked it as if he were handling a woman.

"I know," he said calmly, "that there are some plants that will work if one just believes in them. This one is called the *contra yerba* and it can save you if you are bitten by a black scorpion or a rattlesnake when it wakes up in the spring. It is a plant that lives well here next to the *yerba anis* which, when used right, will save one from a dangerous fever. It is one of those plants which requires a healer, but the one you are standing by, the *matadure*—I have used that one myself for curing skin rashes and wounds. It works almost instantly on most people."

"I can believe what you are saying now, but when it comes to calling birds, I don't see how these herbs explain anything."

"There are some plants here which allow us to tap into other powers, yet it takes great discipline to use them. I don't know what Tsari has learned but it is possible that she did a mushroom ceremony and discovered a voice for calling birds."

"Is it really possible?"

"You were there, so I don't know why you are asking me."

"It was a coincidence, and I know of no world in which it is possible. I don't think she could do it again," I said.

"It is only a child's world to believe what you see."

"Or your Mexican superstitions in this case."

"Don't we remain infants in a dark womb until these things make sense?" he mused.

I'd never seen him so intense and delighted at the same time. Watching him then, walking around in his straw hat, pastel shirt, and tight, bulging jeans—the way he always rocked on his boot heels while talking—I began to share his enthusiasm for his garden.

At the end of the canyon was the goatherd's cabin, a narrow building of small, perfectly arranged logs that held each other in place without a nail.

"I suppose you know," he began, "that I was not called Abulafia until after my father's wife died. My mother and father, bless their unholy union, were never married. She was from the village and when I was young I lived with her. It is not an uncommon situation."

"I didn't know," I replied, and was surprised at this other identity I had failed to recognize—that smile behind the smiles I had been fooled by.

When we were inside, I could see that many small trees had been stripped and fitted together to make perfectly solid walls. The precision of the weaving in wood was more than beautiful; it was nearly impossible to envision the skill, the intricacy of the mind that could patiently complete the task. Even the floor, which was only stones, had been laid without mortar of any kind, and yet there was not a stone out of place, nor any missing in the large stove with a chimney going through the log roof. It was dry and dusty, and the only light came from deerskin windows, the translucent light like that which comes through a drumhead. There were several small rooms which Brito had altered to suit his need for storing supplies and utensils useful for the garden. The disarrangement and the clutter were not appealing, but the whole cabin had a pleasant aura, in the same way that the houses of old people often have a distinct odor of their own, an aura of being a more perfect home than any I had ever been in. It was so containing that nothing outside it seemed to matter very much.

"I feel better about the village, although I don't know why I should," I told Brito when he was ready to leave.

"It is because I brought you here," is all he would say about it.

Seven

Sometimes the country's atmosphere of fatalism and fretful superstition was too much to bear, and I would keep to myself. When I left the States there was a prevalent fatalism about the future, but here the attitude pervaded the present. A few escaped the shadow of it, but to have done so was not necessarily considered a virtue; it was almost sacrilegious. My own escape was the desire to see Tsari again. Everything that Brito knew about her made me wish to as soon as possible, yet I was afraid to go to her village alone. I was hardly paying attention to my work, and when Brito would no longer talk about her, I had no choice but to drive to the village on my own.

I parked in the woods by the village and sent one of the children after her. She had suggested that if I could not find her when I returned, this would be the best thing I could do. The child came back about fifteen minutes later and said he could take me to her. She was waiting at Silvera's house, and I felt somewhat ridiculous at not having gone straight to her.

"I was expecting you," she said. "What took you so long to return?"

"I wasn't sure I'd be welcome."

"You were afraid?" she laughed.

"What's so funny about that?" I said nervously.

"While you were afraid to come see me," she said, "I was wondering if a white man could be good. I have never seen what one looks like; you know, when I want to have a man."

After living on a reservation I was startled not by her frankness, but by her desire to confront me in her father's house. I couldn't refuse, yet it was a rather awkward moment. "We could go into the woods," I said. "It is a lovely day."

"We could go into the town first," she answered, "because it is a lovely day."

"I just came from down there," I said, feeling thwarted.

"But I haven't been there in a long time, and there are things I need."

When the jeep's solenoid died on our way into town after the rough ride through the mountains, she said: "I have to be curious about you; you have a car and you don't know how to make it go." Her words had acquired meanings of their own and I found it hard to distinguish between what was crazy and what was not, for in this mountainous isolation the strange and unexpected were the only identity.

"It's just a cheap part," I said. "We can get another one in town. You don't expect me to be able to fix it out here without another part."

"When a man loses a leg, he carves himself another one. Why don't you just go over to that *palo verde* tree and carve yourself another part?"

"That's just what I'm going to do," I said, and in jest began fishing around under the seat for my ax.

"You think I am going to stay here by the car while you go into town?"

"Yes. If I leave this car on the side of the road, there won't be anything left of it by the time we get back. Some Indian will furnish his house with it."

"I won't. You make me think of the man who came to the village and wanted to hear our stories."

"I don't see how."

"You want someone to wait on you. He wanted us to put down everything we had to do and then tell him stories."

"What stories?" I asked.

" 'What stories?' we asked him."

" 'Your legends and myths,' he told us, 'like how God made the world.' "

" 'We don't know how God made the world,' we told him but it didn't do any good. He wanted us to forget where we were going and tell him stories. 'Well,' we said, 'if you come with us maybe we will tell you about the *komales*.' "

"*Komales* are hearthstones," I said. "Surely he didn't want to go with you to gather stones."

"These are the stones hidden at the mouth of the well. They have been there a very long time."

"What are you talking about?" I asked.

"They are the stones left us by our fathers' fathers. Maybe sometime I will take you to the well. The stones are what we call 'sacred.' They tell stories to those who can read them. They told of how our village would be founded."

"I heard your uncle talk about the 'stones of our fathers.' "

"He was talking about the *komales*," she said.

"Did you tell the man all this?"

"No, he never asked about them again.

"After a while," she continued, "the man spent all his time talking to the clown. The clown told him everything he asked, but no one cared because everyone knew the clown was loco. Finally, the man went away, but before he left he bought the clown's suit from him. It was a very old suit with many shells on it and we were sorry to see it go."

"Maybe we should try rolling this jeep behind the trees," I said, realizing that her story was meant to say she definitely wasn't going to stay with the car. We managed to get it fairly well shielded, and then sat out by the road. One car passed after about three hours, and picked us up. I was beginning to understand about waiting. It was a completely different balance between space and time, and it was not hard to imagine how dealing with such proportions would soon deliver a person into a peculiar state of mind.

In town the variety stores were arrayed Mexican style, all the goods thrown together in piles so that one had to choose by handling each item. There was no way to look around and she plunged in, enjoying herself and examining each piece for flaws, finding them, and starting to bargain, though the few extra pesos would make no difference, since I had offered to pay. I was getting impatient; I finally left her and went for the car part. When I returned she was wrapped around with brightly colored fabrics, long swatches of material to make her deep-colored dresses that barely revealed her ankles. She'd chosen a basketful of metal kitchen utensils, and was straddling it as she examined pairs of shoes; picking each one up, looking at it as if it were impossible to wear, and then going on to another pair. I wanted her to buy whatever she wanted. When she had what she needed, she wanted a lot of trinkets and candy. It puzzled me, unless she had children in mind.

Leaving town with our purchases, we got a ride with a straightforward-looking American. He was on his way to Cucurpe and would pass the jeep before he turned off the highway. The road went through hilly terrain where the pavement was bad and the curves frequent. He acted a little drunk so I didn't offer any conversation. Tsari tried to keep out of his arm's way during his steady maneuvering on the gears. As he kept whipping the truck through the turns, she sat clutching me to keep from being thrown across the seat.

"Can we have a little music?" I asked, hoping that it might calm him down.

"Sure," he said, "I'm beginning to like those sad *rancheros*."

I turned to any station that came in half-clear, and then held on again.

"I just came from church in Douglas," he said, "and I sure feel good. I've been fasting, promised myself not to eat a thing until I met my cousin in Cucurpe."

I didn't know how to respond, or if he were joking.

"I didn't see I had to do the Lord's work until my wife went under; too much temptation in a town like Las Vegas. Had to leave Nevada when she started gambling and drinking," he continued. "But I like my job better here."

"What's that?" I asked half-heartedly.

"My work or my job?"

"I don't know."

"My job's in Douglas, but my work's out here in the mountains. You know one of the ten lost tribes of Israel lives up in those mountains. On long weekends I go looking for them. That is, me and my cousin who lives down here permanent now."

"Any luck?" I asked, wishing that Tsari could understand.

"Nobody's seen these people but my cousin, least no one

I've ever run across. We've been looking for these Indians for a couple of years now. They're real shy."

"Are they hard to find? Or, you just don't know where they come from?"

"Oh, I know where they come from, from Zion, and they wear long robes and carry staffs like in the Good Book. My cousin Jeb, he saw them walking out here once, but we could never find out where they went off to. But we will."

"Let me ask my woman here if she's ever seen them; she comes from around here." I explained to Tsari what this man was after, and her eyes began to laugh.

"Tell him," she said to me, "that if he goes into the hills at Easter time when the *penitentes* are out, when they carry the cross, then he will find just what he is looking for. Maybe they will let him be the thief. No one wants to do that very much."

I quickly saw that this was no dream. Tsari had reminded me that there were still men who relived the Passion right down to the dress and the crucifixion.

"She says," I told our driver, "that she doesn't know." I faced the fact that I could not rob him of his purpose. Once I would have delighted in pointing out his absurdity, and yet he was smiling and Tsari was laughing. We all were, for no good reason.

"With the Lord's help and guidance . . ." he said, and then the mood was finally right; Tsari and I were ready to go off together, somewhere between the dusk and the dawn.

"You know there's a right and a wrong time to lie together," she said. "You will see that."

"I understand now," I said. "It's whenever the mood is with us."

"That would be true, if you wanted to become a father," she returned, smiling, and I assumed she knew I didn't.

Eight

One day I was in one of those moving-vans which had been converted into a bar.

Before me was an empty stage, but everyplace else was cramped with the sounds and smells of men drinking after many hours of work. They had just emerged from the depths of the copper mine, and before they faced the midday ride home, they jammed together for warm drinks and revelry. The sound of the music was nearly deafening. There was no melody, just volume, the roar of machines in a pit mine. It was not the place I thought I'd find my first *entrada* to the world of Brito's garden.

The problem was that the refuse from the mine and its smelter, as Brito had predicted, was contaminating the water supply below the dry lake. We had gone to the mine to speak with some of the company's officials to see what might be done about this. Brito was willing to put up money to devise a better disposal system which would not destroy the crucial water supply. We had a difficult time in the offices, and the officials seemed bored by my technical presentation. They were not from this region and paid attention to us only because Brito was one of the brothers who owned the adjacent ranch. They did not want any trouble and yet were unconcerned about the pollution.

The miners were those mestizos and Indians from surrounding villages who, like us, had a long drive ahead of them to reach their living quarters. I was told that the van was not usually parked by the mine entrance, and that there were many similar vehicles which roamed around the area like carnival wagons, providing entertainment. It was a hot day for the time of year and the bar was doing a heavy business in tequila and mescal.

We had wished to avoid any crowd, and yet neither of us wanted to discuss our frustration, for we did not know what to do next, since I had confirmed that the only water reserves were at the dry lake near the mine. I wasn't sure what this meant for my job, but some delay was inevitable.

After five drinks Brito was ready to leave, but just then the music changed to a slow piece reminiscent of the bands of the 1940s. The curtains fluttered and a tall brownskin woman appeared on the stage, a woman well over six feet tall, taller than most of the men. She wore a black slip and was draped in a long lace shawl that women hereabouts usually wear to church. Brito put his hand on my shoulder, beckoning me to stay a moment longer. "I have heard about her," he said.

She certainly was remarkable. Her hair was dyed red and she wore it pinned up, accentuating her height and the flashing slant of her eyes. She was barefoot and stood silent and motionless, her weight resting on her heels while the men turned to have a look. Everyone was awed by her; I couldn't take my eyes off her, and neither could these men whose eyes were used to the glare of the mine. And soon there was a murmur of remarks as each man reacted, thinking of what he might do if he were alone with her. She silenced them by rising on her toes and gliding into a swirling step which flung the shawl from her shoulders. One had fleeting glances of her smallish breasts through the sheer slip. And as the lace unfurled, the marvel was their black tips jutting out a full two inches. I strained to see if I was imagining things.

Several times she opened her mouth and moved her lips, drawing a breath as if she were about to sing, while slowly she let the lace fall to the floor. She threw her arms into the air and undulated, trying to spin or fly out from her last wrappings. And slowly they began to slide away, coming loose at her narrow shoulders, then down onto her breasts as she bent forward, again and again sweeping the palms of her hands on the floor. Rising abruptly she let everything slip away revealing the startling nipples, holding her pose while she caressed them with her own eyes. Then a turn, her back towards us and the slip falling around her thighs.

She revealed her backside, slender and firm, and her arms moved like eels down her sides. She was all serpentine curves and moves and slowly she was transforming herself into some other, older creature.

I could not guess her age. The dim light and the smoke in the van kept her partially shielded despite her nakedness. She began turning toward us, teasing. Then before us she began to anoint her body, oiling it until it glistened; her red pubic mound seemed ablaze as her slender hands slipped in and out between her legs. I thought it would end like this, a curiosity. But she was not finished with us yet.

From behind the curtain she produced a green vegetable which she handled like a marvelous phallus. Facing us, her long legs wide apart and back arched, she neatly placed it an inch or so inside her, her motions begging the men on. There was uncomfortable laughter in the room. She reached to her breasts and swiftly removed the false nipples and stood in profile to us. The transformation she underwent could not have been more unexpected. She seemed spiteful and triumphant, no longer a serpentine woman but much more like a man, showing us the image of ourselves. And it was hard to accept, hard to assimilate. The men, however, were still enjoying it, caught somehow between the sensual and the lurid. She had not uttered a single sound, and though we had seen flesh it was beyond our touch, like a statue.

She slowly turned around one last time with the vegetable mocking us by its size. She might not even have been aware of us anymore; she appeared to be completely absorbed in her own movement, and her eyes seemed still, looking at no discernible point, a glaze between her and all of us. I decided it was too perverse, that she had gone too far even for a stripper. My one impulse was to leave, to erase her image permanently from my mind. She was neither masculine nor feminine, but definitely one of the old god Yoyontzin's brides, part snake and part bird.

I looked around the van to see if there was an easy passageway to the door. When I looked back toward the stage, she was gone. The loud music blared frivolously again. The men returned to their drinking, more vigorously. I felt I could not have dreamed the entire event, but when we were outside in the bright sunlight I had to blink my eyes several times to adjust and reset my perspectives. When I started to speak, my voice cracked, and I realized I had not said a word for ten minutes.

I could not look at my own erection for several days without feeling bewildered. I learned that she performed under the influence of a drug called *tolache* that is often used as a tobacco, but when swallowed instead, produces a trance-like state, and gives some the power of hypnosis. Brito said that both the vegetable and the drug had once been part of a fertility rite.

Nine

She told me while strolling in the woods with me: "This is the way of untying knots, knots that bind and seal."

"What is?" I had to ask.

"The skipping and jumping of loving."

On the surface, the village was tranquil after the first early snowfall, as if the snow clouds had passed through and left it as it was three hundred years ago. It was almost true, for the drifts had temporarily closed the pass and there was no way down to the mine or to the town; but inside the houses food was short, and everyone was impatient as if they knew a change was at hand.

I was staying at Silvera's house, a sign that his position in the council was improving. Brito, I suppose, had suspected this was the case when he decided I would be of most use at the village. While he was thinking about the water from the mine, I had the chance to see Tsari. Time and again I was asked what it would be like to live on the ranch and farm. I didn't know exactly, but still I was glad to be accepted and live openly with her. I helped Silvera patch his house against the weather while carefully avoiding the headman. I'd had the foresight to bring bags of cornmeal and pinto beans. It turned out that because of Tsari's strange behavior, he and I had to do all the cooking.

I was gathering firewood when I saw her on a large stump, sitting half-naked in the bright sunlight reflecting off the snow which gave a warmth to the winter's day, and singing all the while in a voice so loud I thought she was going to attract the whole village. This was perfectly in keeping with her peculiar activity. She would not eat for several days in a row, and preferred the company of the children, playing with them most of the day and returning to me only at night. Her deep voice was rather pleasant once one got used to its peculiar chanting quality, and I decided not to disturb her. In her song she asked all creatures of the woods where they were going and if she could come along. But the sense was not what carried the song; it was the childlike repetitions and the alternately mocking and serious tone.

When I had spoken to her about the village's future, asking what she thought was best, she answered, "That is men's business," and she would hardly talk about anything other than her dreams and about the places she went in them. All these places were on what she called "the other side," for this was the name of the world where one's dreams, visions, and memory could be held and touched, or so I gathered from her explanation. It wasn't exactly clear, and I suggested that it was a bit frightening because anything could happen there; but she said I was wrong, that it was a place where everything was perfectly ordered. She claimed there was something that she had to know for sure and it meant going on a journey. It didn't make any difference to me, for I understood that she was not going to leave the village.

On my evening trip for firewood she was still sitting in the same place, the snow melted all around her, and it looked like she hadn't moved a muscle. She was no longer singing and I coaxed her to come in. She was happy but almost incoherent. I didn't mind hearing about her journey, but she was convinced that we were talking about the same world we always lived in, not another place, but simply a landscape within the one we usually traveled on. I asked her why she had to be in another phase and she said, "Because you have not reached it yet and I have to find out if there is a way to help you."

I was confused, but this was better than it was when she stopped speaking altogether and entered what appeared to be a rhapsodic fit. This time she refused to come out of the grips of her seizure, and I asked around, trying to find out what was normally done. "Make sure that she keeps warm," I was told. I returned to the house, rekindled the fire, and lay down beside her, cradling her in my arms. It was remarkable how deep her trance was, and she remained oblivious to everything around her. With each breath she struck a chord that turned into a moan, an open and then closed "O" sound, which was so similar to the sound that she made when we had sex that its familiarity plagued me.

The door suddenly burst open without warning, and I was embarrassed to have any witness to our embrace. I rolled over, bewildered, and stared at a woman wrapped in an old blanket, with matted white hair falling across her neck and chest. She had never been around the village before, and I had no idea who she was or what she was doing here.

"How much will you pay me?" she asked while looking keenly at Tsari.

"What for?" I asked in astonishment.

"You must," she said. "She has lost her way and I must retrieve her."

I would have laughed, but there was no weakness in her voice or face, and her voice had the high pitch of a reed played in a round dance. She was very dark and her face did not betray age; rather it had the look of windswept rock, smooth and weathered. I wanted to get up and at the same time wished to seem at ease. I didn't know just how to be polite. Then it struck me, both from this woman's words and appearance, that she was a *curandera*. I remembered what Brito had said about witnessing strange performances. "I will help you," I said, knowing that Tsari would come out of her trance with or without this woman's help, but fascinated by the expectation of what might happen in the meantime.

"You should pay, because it may be your fault," she said. "But it does not matter what you offer, you will pay."

"She is not very sick," I answered, "and I certainly don't see how it could be my fault. But I will do whatever you say."

"She would be gone by tomorrow," the old woman said, and there was something about the piercing squint of her eyes that tended to convince me she knew what she was talking about. "How would you know if she is sick enough to die?"

"There is no fever," I said.

"Once the fever begins, it is too late. You are lucky that I knew of her behavior and that I kept near, for even in the storms I prefer to stay in the woods. I must tell you that most of the white men I have seen were dead."

"Tsari goes to see you when she goes into the high mountains, doesn't she?" I guessed, while trying to ignore her last remark.

"I am called Teresa. I know who you are and will soon see if there is anything to you."

"You know why all this is happening, don't you?" I began, aware that in this old woman I had finally met a person who had the ability to explain. I felt a sudden desire to ask Tsari about this woman whom she had carefully refused to mention, but she lay there, the gleam gone out of her eyes, that focus that I was so fond of. "Why did she do this?" I wondered aloud.

"I have seen it all happen before," Teresa said. "And if it weren't for you I would know just what to do, but you are the one who has no reality for me. I must go on as if you weren't here."

"I do not want anything to happen to Tsari, and you know that is true," I said. I could tell by the way she took this last statement as the words of a simpleton, genuinely felt though they were, that she was not crazy. She was the one person here that nobody ever talked about. And yet people in the hills below talked about true *curanderos* as if they were wizards. I was curious to know if they could be believed.

"I am an old woman," she said, "and Tsari knew that I would choose her, but she is hurrying because she didn't know what to do about you. She was not prepared to go; it will be dark and frightening and there will be a whirling of earth and sky. I must commune with her and then I will know how to find her."

I planned to watch, to see what vital secret this woman possessed that amazed everyone. She produced a dried plant and, after touching Tsari with it, began to grind it into a powder. Her hands worked quickly and soon she asked me to go fetch her some clean snow. When I went outside to get it, I felt better, removed from this woman's presence. But I was drawn back by more than just curiosity. Teresa used the snow to dissolve the powder, and soon had a yellow salve which she applied to Tsari's head. I wanted to know if it were a stimulant and she told me only that it was called the *yerba del pasmo*. She said that Tsari could not hear her until the fit was alleviated. The herb would not cure her, but it would make it possible for us to speak with her in the place where she was.

"Where is that?"

"On the other side," she said, "out there along the passages to the center where the green tree of abundance is, in the home of souls."

I was not convinced, and yet I understood she was going to probe Tsari's subconscious. At least, I was going to learn what it was that was driving her to endanger herself—I would have the old woman's interpretation. Teresa knelt down by her and opened her coat, unbuttoned her skirt, and began examining Tsari's belly. She then handed me a dried fungus and told me to eat it. I refused. She said, "Eat it or leave for good." It wasn't an idle threat and I complied. It was like eating chalk. When Teresa placed her hands on the belly, she suddenly looked at me with alarm and horror.

"What is it?" I demanded.

But she only howled, a sound somewhere between that of a wolf and a lion. When she finally stopped, I began to see more clearly, and what I saw was that Teresa's hands were taking on a way of their own as they slowly rubbed across Tsari's navel, kneading her flesh. The fingers were long and slender and did not fit a woman with thick, short limbs. Their texture was almost barklike, gnarled knuckles and wrinkled calluses. Only her palms were smooth, and all her strength seemed to come from the quickness in those hands. They had told her something about Tsari which had shocked even her and I could not even guess what it was.

The hands remained fixed to their task, but Teresa now began to sway and hum with no apparent melody audible. The sound became shrill, the hum grew clearer. It was singing, and the words were not clear, but sounds said over and over again. Soon the sounds and the movement of her hands joined in a steady rhythm. The hands seemed to disappear into Tsari's skin.

The old woman's face was contorted, but not in pain; a concentration rather, and there was a heat of inner lights that actually made the fire glow brighter, casting an eerie phosphorescence across the earthen walls. Within this presence I could feel a spiritual power that was beyond the power of perception, and the warmth of a fire came within me.

Ten

The next morning, though they were both gone, the night had been so intense, and the mushroom so effective, that the experience kept repeating itself.

The colors of the fire grew behind my closed eyes like multicolored bands twirling around a six-pointed star, and I heard Teresa digging a hole with her bare hands.

Teresa: "I am an old woman   I have seen the whirlwind in the mountains   I have held the whirlwind in my hands   These are the hands   These are the hands which find the herbs   You are He who brings forth the colors   You are He who speaks with the light of day   Here is the woman who is not yet old   She does not know where to turn   She has two feet   She goes in two directions   She has begun the journey back   She has become a child   Here is her lover

He holds her like a baby She is gone She goes for help
She is lost She pulled her fingers through her hair She
held the earth in her hands She rubbed her belly She
opened the passageway Her soul flew out Her soul was un-
accustomed to the dark Through this hole I fly, through
this hole I go to the center of her earth."

There was no perceptible change in Tsari, and I don't
think she was aware of our presence. I tried to watch carefully, but it took a great effort to focus on one thing at a
time, so strong were the moods of the mushroom. The more
obscure regions of my mind were now the more lucid. I was
experiencing Tsari's despair at trying to reach the other side.
I saw the many colors of her emotions and each was at-
tached to a different tree. I saw myself as a threat. A threat
looked very much like a cloud. In this cloud there was
nothing. Soon this cloud was filled with hundreds of vacant
fish eyes. I wished that she would look at me but her eyes
remained closed and her hands motionless.

Teresa whistled. "Do not be frightened my child   I am
calling you" She whistled once more. "I am she who looks
for the spirit I am she who searches Where has the spirit
sent you Where are you hiding It is dark in the north It
is dark in the south It is dark in the east It is dark in the
west I am she who sees around corners I am she who
looks through mountains I can see into the dark places I
see a shape lost in the dark cavern I see it is frightened
It quivers like a small dog Your soul is yapping at me Your
soul is baring its puppy teeth I whistle to it I call for it

from the light We will go on living in the company of our people We will go on living in our homes I will continue with my children I will continue with my mother Strong is the cord which binds us Strong is the leash I bind you with."

When the old woman stopped I was sure that Tsari would speak. I knelt beside her and waited for her to awaken and tell me why she persisted in ignoring us and why she would force herself to a breakdown. I was now sure that she had had a nervous collapse and that she had purposely brought it upon herself.

"Now," Teresa said, "what are you waiting for?"

I just stared at both of them and felt sleepy.

"I have found her. Do you want her back or don't you? I can't do it alone. It is going to require all our strength. She must hear you too."

"I am right here."

"Tell her what you feel. Make her believe you."

"I am sorry. If it is my fault, I am sorry," was all I could say.

"Call her back," the old woman screamed at me. "Can't you see her?"

I tried to close my eyes and see what Teresa was seeing.

"Open your eyes and look here through the hole."

As I did this I saw something I recognized. It was the ledge of a canyon. I began to think that Tsari was there and that she had to be coaxed off the ledge. It was night in the canyon and it seemed that the trail actually went along a vertical axis. "Here I am," I yelled. "Come on up."

"She can't hear you," Teresa whispered.

"I will love you; you know I will love you. I have never known a woman like you. We shall spend our nights together. When I hear you speak, I will know you are all right." I tried to speak like Teresa in a penetrating voice, but I felt foolish, and yet relieved, for I found this ritual much more satisfying than just watching her inert body. At least I was doing something for myself.

Teresa: "There is a sign Tsari I don't know what will happen There is a good sign Come back Do you hear us calling you Let the yerba work It has passed through the hands of the earth I pulled it up It is the strand I am the shore You are the one I have chosen It will all pass on to you I set up my virgin tree gourd I have your soul with me I have taken you by the hand We shall come together You are the fire for my old loins See I touch your breasts See I hold your furrow See I kiss you See we have one tongue . . ."

I was no longer able to concentrate. There was something the old woman did that I could not see. Now she too had fallen into a trance and so intense was her feeling that her eyes were focused on no object around us. As she—it seemed her presence left the room—fell away from me also, I began snapping back into a more conscious state. Not that I could understand where they were or what they were doing but I could watch their bodies. Teresa's lips were still moving but they only produced occasional sounds, and the mumbling sounded something like prayer voices in the distance.

I was no longer judging, rather I was watching intently. Teresa was shaking, quivering as if from a great chill, and Tsari was lying very quietly; even her moaning had ceased. Then it began to turn. Their hands were joined, and the shuddering seemed to be moving, was actually moving from one body to the other. Tsari began to shake slightly, and Teresa's shuddering subsided a bit. Teresa's eyes closed, and Tsari's opened; Teresa was moaning, and her body was losing its rigidity, turning much calmer, more somnolent. Tsari began tossing, shaking her legs. I tried to hold her steady, but her body ignored my pressure and turned its energy elsewhere. For a moment she sat up. I thought she was going to speak, so intent did she look, and I felt her eyes focus upon me in recognition. I jumped up, and though I don't know how to dance, I was dancing a kind of jig and singing, "Here we go round . . . Here we go round the mulberry bush, the mulberry bush, the mulberry bush." I thought Tsari would get up and join me. Instead, she lay back down and the rapidity of her breathing subsided. Her eyes were open. Both women were lying facing me, their eyes open toward me, but looking past me to some invisible world of their own. As one inhaled, the other would exhale. Their synchronization was as regular as a machine. Occasionally, Teresa would make a jerk of some kind, a knee or an elbow, and a second later Tsari would follow suit. It was not that movement was jumping from one body to another; I was witnessing an exchange. The old woman looked younger, and Tsari older. Nothing else happened. They both lay like this for a long time.

Finally my legs would not support me any more, and it was far too hot in the house. I went outside and remembered looking into the sky among the stars, searching for something which I must have lost up there. I kept looking into the star clusters, even after I lay down on the leaves and branches piled against the wall. Outside there were only two things, my sleep, which looked like a bowl of stars, and the breathing of the two women alternating in rhythm. The drug inside the mushroom acted as an amplifier so that their breathing began to pound like heartbeats. The sounds went "Oh-we, Oh-we, Oh-we." They grew fainter, the beats shorter and shorter. They grew more intermittent—until they were both erased. A winter night's crisp silence.

I woke up lying comfortably in the snow about forty yards in back of the house. I didn't know how I had gotten there or when, but the mad blaring of the goats startled me into awareness.

Eleven

The hacienda loomed up against the storm blowing down from the north, an ancient fortress beneath the vast grayness covering the sky. Swirling clouds drifted over the hills, while everywhere the wind ripped and bellowed and the whole plain felt deserted, stripped down to the bare white bones of lost cows. The water ran along the dry ground trying to soak in, but even this storm season was hardly enough to reverse the periodic drought.

I had no choice but to escape from the mountains before it permanently closed the pass, and what I needed was rest and the chance to find out what Brito knew about Teresa. She and Tsari were off together, caught somewhere else in the solitude of the storm. I kept thinking about my hands in the light of what Teresa had done. I had never paid much attention to them before. They were good at drawing charts and at loving—when they had a desire of their own.

When I pulled through the open gate, the only people in sight were a vaquero and one of the girls. The man was mounted and leaned low over the mane to speak with her. The horse kept rearing and made their courting difficult. But there was no need for him to keep spurring it to impress her, and to strike a pose.

"Bueno."

"Bueno, Señor," he answered above the pounding generator.

"Where are you off to?"

"There's a cow twinning, Señor, and one of the drivers said she was in trouble."

"Where are all the trucks?"

"They are either stuck or they have gone to pull out the ones that are caught in the mud of this rain."

"You'll freeze talking," I said, "or those calves will freeze waiting for you."

"It will be cold tonight," he said and his voice indicated that he didn't care, that it was an affectation of mine to care about the weather.

I went into the inner courtyard by the main house and it unnerved me to see a large sedan with Mexico City plates parked by the door. I wished to have Brito to myself, or else to be alone. A hulking man in a business suit was examining a wall of family portraits in the long hallway.

"You're the watershed engineer," he said.

"Hydrologist," I said.

"We've been waiting for you," he said without irritation and yet implying that I was late.

"I didn't know."

"It doesn't matter. I'm Alberto, Brito's brother." I had assumed this, although he did not resemble his brother at all, cut from an entirely different cloth, and at least ten years older.

"I've got a long name and everyone here calls me J.P.," I said.

"Brito and I have been talking and I am hoping to have a big job for you here. Let's go to the dining room."

I was quite tired after being up most of the night and from the rough drive, but I had no polite alternative to joining him. The formal dining area, which was not often used, was a long two-story room with enormous old hand-carved furniture. It was usually draped and dark, but this afternoon it was lit with candles and the twenty-foot table set with silver and fine crystal. Brito and another man sat talking at the far end of the table. A woman sat in one of the high-backed chairs against the wall, leaning on a table set against a tall, narrow window. She did not respond to our entrance and continued staring at the wind bending the trees as I was introduced to the man, a wealthy grower from the Culiacan area. He was a slight man with curly gray hair, and wore a custom-made suit. At a glance, I thought the woman was with him, for she was dressed in fashionable clothes.

The issue at hand was the water basin near the mine,

and my charts and maps were out on the table. Brito and I had decided that the water could be pumped out at a rate capable of supplying one thousand acres of fertile land around the mouth of the barranca. I supposed that the plans had to be approved by his brother, but I didn't know what the grower was here for and could only guess that he was going to advise them both about profitability.

As we ate, I learned that Alberto had a completely different plan in mind. He wanted to grow maize suitable for livestock so that the cattle would be subject to less random grazing. It was the continuing drought which worried him, and the depletion of the grazing land. His main hope was to keep the ranch self-sufficient, but my mind wasn't on this problem and I had no desire to be with these people.

"Can it be done?" he asked me.

"I think so," I said and paused, realizing that I was tired enough to agree to anything.

When I'd first arrived I envisioned setting up a well-designed irrigation system that would do pretty much what Alberto had in mind. I foresaw a modern operation where the ranching and farming were integrated. It was what the future held for this area, and I had a chance to establish my reputation among the ranchers, and there were many wealthy ones. So I forced myself to listen to what Alberto was saying.

"We would need enough water for a farm to support around two thousand head. What do you think?" Alberto asked me.

"It would be a big project," I said, and began to think how it had been done elsewhere.

"I'd like to know if we could do it here."

I looked over to Brito to see if I could get any clue to how he wanted me to answer, but he was entertaining the woman, charming her. I couldn't quite understand what he found in a woman like her, who belonged in the city. Irritated by her genteel flirting, I was left to reason on my own.

I made a hasty decision, and said: "I don't think it would be an advisable thing to do."

"We have the opportunity," Alberto said, "to buy the necessary farming equipment and most of the pumping hardware at a very reasonable price, because of my friend here. I would not pass up this chance unless I was absolutely sure we didn't have the water. You know, we have a lot of land to draw from."

"I know," I said. "But there's barely enough water for what Brito and I have been talking about."

"You would not be alone in your opinion? Others would confirm what you have said?" Alberto demanded.

"That's my opinion," I said and for the moment was spared any further explanation by the women who brought in the coffee and started clearing the table. Without having decided to, in my own mind I was supporting Brito's intention of moving the village . . . because when the time ran out it would be either an Alberto or a Brito who would be in charge. I preferred Brito, even while he was so entranced by this woman who had come up with his brother, for whom she worked. In an ordinary way she was quite beautiful with her vivid makeup on. The grower started asking me what I had been doing lately. I replied that I had been in the mountains.

"Oh, you've been hunting up there. I hear it's a good area for bighorn sheep."

"Yes," I said, "I suppose that's so."

"If it weren't for this weather, I'd like to get up there, myself."

"It's lovely," I said, and there was nothing else I could say to him. I wasn't sure just who was aware of Brito's plans for the village, or of any of Brito's intentions with his greenhouse. I was trying to think in two different worlds at once and it exhausted me.

As soon as possible I excused myself and went along the exterior passageway to my room. As tired as I was, I wasn't ready to go in yet, and sat down on the step outside watching the storm. I thought about why I had come here in the first place and of the opportunity I so casually passed by, for in a period of normal rainfall Alberto's plan was completely feasible. It was a gamble I would have approved of if Brito had suggested it. But the image that I held to now, the one that had taken hold of me, was of the Opatas camped by the river and farming in a way that had evolved between the people and the land over centuries. I saw in my mind Silvera praying over the crops, and a woman dancing for fertility.

So my decision at the table was not based on whim, and

although inadvertent, it came, I believe, from that other order of things—the one where an old woman chanted by the firelight to recover the soul of the woman I was beginning to love.

I went inside feeling content, and there was really no purpose in asking Brito to explain what had happened to me at the village.

Twelve

After two weeks of scattered thundershowers, when the first cloudless day came I decided the weather itself was an omen, and it was time to find Tsari again. I felt I was missing something by not being with her, even if her company was not always easy to take. It was a fascination much like watching the stripper perform, where it was hard to take my eyes off what was going on no matter what my feeling was.

Brito still wanted me to spend as much time at the village as possible so that I would have time to explain his ideas about farming on the ranch, and also to know the people who were in favor of it. It was the way I best fit into his plans, he told me, and I agreed. It was Tsari who appeared reluctant, and didn't invite me to stay until I suggested that we go see the place where the stones were kept.

"I would like to see what makes them sacred," I said.

"If you can't, then I may hate you afterwards."

"Then let's find a suitable place for something else. It's been a while since we were alone."

"No, let's go and see what happens, because any time may be your entrance. When I go I am either afraid or it is a sacred time. The spirit depends on the place; I will show you."

"I'm sure I will like it," I said.

"It affects everyone differently. It is beautiful but it is not always kind."

"I'm in a good mood, I think."

"We will see, for it was not so kind to me the first time I went there."

"How can a place be kind? Is it dangerous?"

She led me down to a trail at the entrance of the barranca which could be followed if one went with his back to the cliff and shuffled sideways. The water, after the rains, covered this ledge, but Tsari felt it wouldn't be more than a few inches deep. She went first, and taking off my boots and tying them over my shoulders, I cautiously followed her. At first, the going wasn't too bad, and indeed there was a solid ledge below us. Soon, however, the strain of bracing our backs against the cliff took its toll on our endurance. We could not speak without shouting at the top of our lungs, and as it became more difficult I questioned why I was doing this.

We stopped frequently but this hardly provided relief,

since there was no room to turn our bodies. The only compensation was that, as I watched the other bank with its cliffs jutting out into the river, I knew it was absolutely impassable. Boulders in the middle of the river coupled with the steepness of the canyon precluded travel by boat. Thus we were taking the only possible route upriver. The first time we rested, I checked my watch to see at what rate we were progressing, and discovered, to my dismay, that somehow I had smashed the crystal and the hands against the rock. Angry at myself, I tore it off my wrist and gave it to the river. Then we went on again.

To add to our difficulties, the coldness of the water numbed our feet and we lost our sensitivity to the quality of the footing below. We were in the shadow of the cliff with the sun behind us and could see it playing brilliantly off the multicolored lichens on the cliff wall opposite us. It was light without warmth. There was no way to change the situation now, but I began to feel that it was not right for Tsari to be leading the way. I wanted to be leading, to be in command of the situation, to demand that she let me. We were in such a narrow spot along the ledge that, as thirsty as I was, I could not risk reaching down for water, and the ledge was mounting steadily higher.

The fact was that I was in no condition to take the lead, was experiencing a kind of fatigue, and in response my mind became more alert, focusing on every sensation of the rock surface. But soon such attention began to defeat itself and turned into an unbearable pressure. Tsari didn't seem to notice my condition or maybe she thought it would be useless to acknowledge it. The ledge we were on was now some twenty feet above the water level, and I had to contend with the vertigo of height accentuated by the swirling of the water. I tried not to look down. So tense were my muscles that I felt at any moment I would explode. What was Tsari going through? She said nothing and did not look at me. And why hadn't she emphasized the difficulty we would encounter in reaching the sacred place? I was actually angry at her, and this seemed to calm me down, the excess energy of my fear being burned up by my anger.

Gradually my tension unwound as my muscles and ligaments grew numb from the strain upon them. But as I regained my composure the ledge became more dangerous. There were gaps in it large enough for a person to fall through which we had to leap across without shifting from our sideways position. At one point, a sharp sliver of rock behind my head and the largest crevice beneath, I stood poised trying to reach one foot to the next part of the ledge. It wouldn't reach and my balance wavered in the thundering of the water, my toes slipping on the rock until I was forced to give up my solid footing and spring forward in one tense instant with no hold on either ledge. Then one small foothold was enough. The ledge began to tilt downward and we were able to move faster toward another one which extended out into the river.

With relief, we both fell into a small pool of sand in a hollowed-out part of the rock that provided the twenty feet of our salvation. It was our first chance to stretch our muscles, and there was no need to talk about how we had felt; our relief was indication enough.

"There is just one more bend to go around," Tsari said, and I could hardly hear her, for with the wane of the internal throbbing in my ears came the deafening roar ahead of us. I suspected a waterfall.

"In about ten days I'll be able to go around that bend," I said.

Tsari said that we would lose strength by resting too long and started to go ahead along the main ledge. But as I began to get up, rocks came sliding down the cliff above us. It was just sand and pebbles at first and so we kept going, hoping to make it into the wider part of the canyon ahead of us. I heard crashing, the first loud rocks hitting the water, and for a moment I froze. And trying to hold on, my grip failed me, and I fell toward the water at the same instant that Tsari dived in.

The river was cold and swift but not deep. I touched bottom when the water bubbled over my eyes, and I was able to bounce up—but not get in a position to swim. I didn't see Tsari, and prayed the rocks hadn't hit her. My clothes quickly became heavy with water, holding me back. The very canyon walls with their red tones swirled around me, and it was all I could do to stay afloat. The river was dark and thick as if dyed by the red-earth clay, and I kept going under, holding my breath, knowing I had to keep upright.

It was slow going and each step depended on getting a foot-hold at the bottom.

The center of the river was suddenly too deep, forcing me to swim. I tried it under water but I couldn't see and fright kept me from holding my breath. I came up even with the rocks and was sure that I would be thrown against them. I didn't know what the water held and I anticipated that at any moment I would feel some sharp pain; I didn't know where. Then my leg stung and I reached down to find it was only a branch that struck me. I came up again, whirled around, caught sight of Tsari to the left of me, saw rocks striking the water, went under again, collided with a rock, and then I was caught up by the current after losing my footing completely. My floundering around began to strike me as comical although I was furious at myself, and the swirling current was sweeping me right back to the ledge.

Tsari scrambled back onto it while I waited, treading water in front of her. Her dress was ruined and even her breasts, which had slipped free, were scarred with mud. There was a small trickle of blood running down her foot, for she had cut herself in the water. We were both too drenched and shaken to continue on, and agreed it would be best to go again another time when the will of the canyon was more in our favor.

As we approached the area at the base of the barranca again, where the river came out of the cliffs and went through a small valley filled with peach trees, I thought there was yet a chance to retrieve the day. The beauty of the spot was matched only by its total seclusion. Tsari went to the bank of the river and tried to rinse herself clean without undressing. I had an irresistible urge to seduce her; a foolish one I suppose, for if I'd had the sense to make the right connections I would have known that it was the wrong time. It should have been obvious from what I had experienced in the canyon, but then we shared our house of gloom much of the time.

I was not ever aware of anything that would lead me to suppose she was modest, and I went over to her. After some coaxing she agreed to let me massage her back to relieve the fatigue of the ledge. She lay on her stomach while I worked my hands up and down beneath her blouse. I unfastened it and, after kneading her shoulders until they relaxed, began running my finger up and down her spine until she shuddered from the chill it gave her. When I began to kiss the back of her neck, she quickly realized what I was about and warned me to quit.

"I do not want you today," she said.

"I have waited all day," I said.

"No," she replied, but she allowed me to continue caressing her body.

"Oh, why are you doing this to me?" she asked as she forced herself onto her side. "I don't want you now."

I tried to convince her that it would not be harmful to have sex at this moment, but her fear was built on a mood which could not be questioned. We had succeeded in reaching that frustration where we were hurting each other, to no avail.

"Is it the privacy of your body or your beliefs that you don't wish to share now?" I wondered.

"It is because I care for you and wish to protect you," she said.

"But there is no real danger," I said.

"It is already too late. What shall I do with you?"

I didn't have to accept the ominous tone in her voice, not in such a beautiful spot as the peach grove, and yet my confidence had been undermined twice in one day. She turned away from me with a harsh look on her face, and with her hair wet and dripping she looked austere enough to begin with. And on that clear afternoon it was a bleak moment when I felt that in some way I would have to atone for my inability to understand.

Thirteen

"It was not harder for you than for me."

"But you were in your home while I was between your world and mine, and did not understand how things were handled."

"Do you think anyone here will believe you if you say that only you were confused? Each time I left the village I wondered to myself: should I go up into the mountains to see Teresa or should I go down to the ranch? Some nights I would cry when I could not decide between you."

"How did you know what to do?"

"It was my body that told me. Sometimes it longed for you and sometimes for the powers of Teresa."

"I had moments when I felt you were torn, but the feelings were vague. I could not be sure. I did not know how to follow those intuitions then, even though the love kept getting stronger."

"There is a power of loving which brings out the most in us. It was not desire alone that would make me tremble when you touched me. When all our attention has focused on it, a love can be binding and deadly."

"When I had the power, you felt it yourself. You obeyed even when the pain was almost killing you, for my hands were possessed."

"You had the craft of the hands. It was your gift—one you didn't know you had until it was a matter of what you loved most.

"Yes, I suppose that is true but how can I explain this? For there will always be a great suspicion of white men here."

"You don't know what language to use. You are the leaf on the border between two worlds. It will be a mixture, I think, and the time will choose which—you."

"It seems my whole life has taken less energy than these last months. I feel that I have no past, and that I have never been anywhere else but here. It is very hard to talk about."

"You still think it was harder for you than for me."

Tsari wanted me to leave her alone for a time, and there was a great deal of tedious work left for me to do if Brito's irrigation plan would be possible. I had to develop a system of pumping stations and, because of the mine, had to combine them with a filtration procedure. It meant returning to the States to order equipment, and it was almost Christmas before I saw her again. She showed up without any warning, asking that I take her to the seashore. She needed to find certain magical objects for Teresa.

"Like what?" I asked, for I had no desire to go to the sea.

"Like the shell that has the sound of the sea, and the sky-blue corals," she said.

Brito decided to go with us and then changed his mind, leaving me obligated to go. There seemed to be no good reason and yet if she meant one thing she often said another. Neither the ranch nor the village suited her purpose, since she wanted to tell me what my fatherhood meant to her. It was not normal and she chose a small fishing village not far below Yuma where her people had traditionally gone for salt pilgrimages. It was remote from those political quarrels which surrounded her village. They were not her main concern anyway.

We had just come out of the water and were letting the sun and sea breeze dry our bodies.

"When you look on my body," she said, "I feel your eyes touch me, but also I know when you are pleased and when you are not."

"You are always attractive to me," I said.

"That is not true. I know when you wish I were made like a white woman, when you think I am too fat and my body sticks out in the wrong places. Well, I will be much broader, for now I am carrying your child."

I had hoped that this was true, believing that it now would bring us closer, and that she would come to live with me. When she told me I was so excited I just sat down on the sand and looked at her with completely loving awe.

"You don't have to say anything," she said, "for I had chosen your face long before you ever saw me."

"I thought it was because you wanted to be with me," I said.

"Maybe I do," she said. "But it is our custom to keep a baby at its mother's house."

"But your mother is dead," I said, "and there are different customs. Where I come from a woman will live at the house of the man when she carries his child."

"That's ridiculous," she said. "What if he leaves her?"

"So that's what you were afraid of," I said.

"Why should I be afraid of that?" she said. "I have lived at the house of my mother all my life."

"Sometimes I don't know you at all," I said.

"Once, I saw your face on an Indian man, an Apache I think, when we were at a ceremony. I couldn't find him when the drinking began, but I didn't have to go looking for him again, because very soon you came to the hill. He too looked like a scarecrow."

"It was just a coincidence," I said. "You are attracted to a certain kind of man."

"After my first child died inside me, I very carefully chose the face for the next father; otherwise I would have never spoken to you. I wanted a man whose eyes looked in every direction at once. I knew he would have to have a lean, hard face with great hollows between his bones."

"But I am not like that," I said.

"That is because you don't see yourself clearly."

"I feel very lonely when you talk this way," I said, "because I can look like only one person at a time and I want to be only that person."

"Once when I was at the sacred place and stood before the *komales* an eye opened up for me, and through it I saw the whole tribe of faces. I saw spirits choosing their faces and I saw people living out the life of their face. There were not many different faces after all, and the slight differences were easily forgotten. I would know a person by his inner face and then I would know what his life was. Once I saw your face on a rabbit."

"I am not a rabbit," I said, "and what I want is for us to live together now that there will be a baby."

"I thought you would say that," she said. "That is why I did not tell you right away and that's why I have been trying to explain. Because the baby is inside me, it is mine and not yours."

"I don't want to talk about it anymore," I said. "I just want you to know that I am very happy that it is my child inside you."

"Are you?" she asked.

I got up and went off to be alone at the edge of the beach. I wanted to think out what she was telling me, for I wasn't sure she wasn't making it all up. She might have been trying to tell me that once the baby was inside her I was no longer very important. But then she might have had a completely different intention. Her words may have been meant only to explain the way things were on the other side and that nothing had changed between us. "Nothing has changed between us," I told myself as I threw water-smoothed stones out towards the wreck of an old boat aimlessly rocking on the surface of the ocean.

When she came over to me she was wearing one of her long dresses. She wanted to know if I was mad at her.

"Doesn't matter," I said.

"It does," she said, "because there is only one way I can stay with you. You must become like me so that we can live together. I have a story to tell you which Teresa told me, and then I will show you what will happen."

"I'm not sure I want to know."

"You must listen. A man loses his wife. He does not sleep for many nights and then he decides he will follow her wherever she goes. He keeps a vigil over her grave until one night she rises and begins her sleepwalk to the strange land which lies inside the mountains. 'My love and death,' he exclaims, 'am I really a witness to this?' It is so, and he follows her without betraying his presence until she comes to a bridge that crosses a deep gorge. When his wife sees him, she tells him he cannot cross because he has put his fingers into too many women and found them attractive. 'You will fall in and become a snake,' she warns. But this man has not accepted her death and has found words of power to steady the bridge, for he has denied the abyss.

"On the other side," she continued, "he sees that his wife has entered a scorched plain where the plants are shriveled and full of thorns. And on this plain a great round dance has begun. As he approaches the dancers, they stop and complain that there is a great smell because of him, and ask him to leave. Then his wife comes over to him and says that he can stay with her only if he changes and becomes like her. But the man does not want to die. 'Then you must learn to travel in both worlds,' she says. 'You came here once so you should be able to come here again, only next time you must get rid of your smell.' The man realizes he doesn't know exactly how he was able to follow his wife and certainly does not know how to get rid of the smell he carries. He sets out to explore the region he finds himself in, for he does not believe he will be able to return if he leaves."

"Then you feel that we will be married?"

"No. That's not it."

"Then it's not our story."

"Yes, it is about us. You know that I have been to the other side and that you must follow me."

"Please," I said, "I understand it is a story but you and I are real and alive. We can talk about these other worlds but we can't live in them." But even as I said this I was feeling better, for just hearing her tell the story had soothed me.

"But we both must be able to go to the other side and get

our instructions. You must learn how real it is and how to get there. For this reason Teresa gave me a salve she made in the mountains."

"Is it a drug?" I asked. "If so I don't want it."

"It's just a plant that keeps you calm."

"I am calm," I said.

"No, you are not. I can tell when you are feeling uneasy. Please, let us both use it to be together."

She leaned over, as if trying to soothe me, put her hand over my forehead, and pressed her palm against my skin. It left a mint-cool feeling. We sat awhile facing each other as the waves came past us and then fell back again. She opened her legs, enticing my sight into the soft world between them. And then she did something I felt was quite odd. She moved slightly as if to curl one leg under her while bracing her weight with her hands. Then as a woman might rise after a fall, she stretched her hands toward me. I received her and when she could lower her body on me, felt her flesh-warmth engulfing me.

"Will you always be good to me?" She smiled, but I couldn't answer since for a long second I was sure that I saw two of her. That is, there were two figures on the wet sand beside me.

"Don't stop," she cried, and I could feel myself inside her, the moistness and all, while I could plainly see that she was still kneeling three feet away from me as if she were about to rise. The water rushed between us and over us, curled with a white froth, and cooled our embrace. I tried to rub the salve off but it had turned to perspiration. My eyes were afire from a sharp, penetrating mint that burned like the light reflecting off the waves.

"Love both of me," she murmured and I knew that she too was under the influence of this unexpected gift from Teresa. It seemed we were moving while the beach and the ocean merged into an endless white expanse, and there were two pure sources of feeling, as if I had touched what my image was doing in a mirror. Even if the sky was under me, the being-inside-her was real enough, and I stopped caring if my senses or feelings were true to my past experiences, for I was about to have an orgasm in two places at once.

Fourteen

One morning after I returned Tsari to the village, I lay in bed half-awake with the distinct feeling that I was being watched by someone in the room. I had been trying to center myself, to separate what was real from what wasn't. While I wasn't afraid of the unreal, I wasn't going to give up my ability to distinguish between what I felt and what I did, even if it made it more difficult to deal with Tsari. To keep from giving in to that impulse to turn around quickly, I thought about loving her and about Brito's surprise when I told him that she and I were going to have a baby. I remembered the excitement upon returning, an eagerness to go back to work, feeling that Tsari would soon join me at the ranch.

I fell back to sleep and began to dream. It was one of

those light, vivid dreams where I hardly realized I was asleep. I was out walking in the mountains on a loose gravel path and my footsteps made a crunching sound. I assumed it was my footsteps even though it was clear that the sound was coming from far below me. I finally looked down and felt like I was having somebody else's dream, for in the ravine below me were mud-caked men with black eyeholes and rounded heads whose bodies wavered, disjointed in a grotesque walk. I tried to hide but had trouble retaining my balance, and accidentally I started a shower of rocks. As soon as they saw me they began calling to me, their arms outstretched, reaching toward me in supplication.

"Where are you going?" they asked.

"Nowhere," I answered.

"Then come with us," they replied.

"I don't know you," I said. Although the ravine was too steep to climb they began to come toward me, ignoring my fear. In desperation I began to push oval boulders toward them. As they rolled down, the ground became diffused with a yellow glow and yet the men kept coming, seeming to float among the boulders.

I wanted to run but my legs wouldn't carry me, and at the same time I felt I was about to fall into their midst. The ground was shaking beneath me. "I don't know you," I cried.

"What are you talking about?" a voice said.

"What are you doing here?" I said when I turned around and saw Tsari. She was kneeling by the edge of the bed so close that I could feel her breath.

"I came to see you," she said.

"How long have you been watching me sleep?"

"Some time," she said. "You still do not understand, do you?"

"What are you talking about?"

"You are becoming a problem," she said. "At first, it was fine but now you make it very difficult. Why do you resist hearing what I tell you?"

"I don't," I said.

"I love you," she whispered with a stern expression.

"Why?" I blurted out. It was a question I never meant to ask.

"Because you take care of me. I never thought a man would do that for me. I was going to be like Teresa and live alone."

"Then stay with me here instead of going back into the mountains."

"I love you even if I shouldn't," she said. "I wish you would understand that there are other things that I must do."

"You are trying to tell me something," I said.

"I came to tell you that I am leaving this morning. Teresa and I are going to the south."

"How long will you be gone?" I asked.

"A few days," she said.

"That's fine," I said laughing. It didn't seem necessary for her to be so serious since we were usually apart for much longer periods of time.

"Then why were you so at odds with your dream?"

"Say that again," I said.

"What were you afraid of?"

"How did you know what I was dreaming?"

"I was watching you."

"I was talking about it in my sleep?"

"You were talking in English."

"But you don't understand English."

"That's true," she said and I lay back on the pillow, closing my eyes, astounded that she had the ability to read my moods, even when I was asleep.

She left quietly, before I was ready to get up. When I did, I went out to piss and could hardly concentrate on what I was doing. There was a burning sensation and it was actually difficult to urinate. The urge was overpowering and finally I was able to. I blamed this on being so distracted by what Tsari had done that I couldn't control my body, my involuntary muscles.

But the burning sensation persisted for several days and I remembered how I had felt after I'd seen the stripper. This time Brito was no help whatsoever. He could not explain what was wrong with me.

"I warned you about the traditions," he said, "that time we went to my greenhouse."

"Why didn't you tell me about Teresa then?"

"I don't think you would have believed me. You had to see her for yourself. You did not have to see Tsari again after the birds if you did not wish to be involved with such things. It was your decision."

As the pain got worse I became convinced that the problem was not psychological. I finally understood that I had a bladder infection. But by this time I was too uncomfortable to drive and asked one of the hands to take me to the clinic in town. Riding on the unpaved road was too intensely painful and I had to return to the ranch.

I went to bed and Brito came in to check on me. I reminded him of what he had said about modern medicine, saying that if I didn't know there was a pill for my condition, I would be sure I was going to die.

"How do you know you won't?" he retorted.

"Don't joke," I said, and even the words hurt.

"We may not have the medicine here in this area."

"Then we could get it from the States."

"It and the doctor might arrive after we have buried you. Then I would have to pay for the visit."

"If you make me laugh," I said, "then I will die." I was beginning to get dizzy, weak from the toxic state of my body and from the agonizing sweating the pain caused. I could imagine thousands of tiny white crystals growing in my tubes; then they began to fill the room like a fog. I let my mind wander to divert myself, for I knew the expected thing was to grin and bear it. Everything around me smelled and I made Brito open the window so I could get a breath of clean air. I began to wonder aloud what happened if a person's bladder burst. After a while he said I was babbling and that it would be better if I rested. He gave me a tab of morphine and left. I began to worry that the doctor would not come. I slept off and on, and am not sure that what happened during the night was not another dream.

Tsari came into the room and closed the window. Then, she made me leave the bed and lie on the floor wrapped in a wool blanket. She spoke in a voice which was like her own, but much more deliberate; the pitch was controlled to hold my attention, and I had no choice but to submit to each of her commands. I noticed that she was sweating and that her clothes were torn. She never asked any questions and yet she carried on as if she had been with me all the time.

"I have been running," she said, "I had a pain in my *muhs*, and could not piss."

I was quite calm and asked her to get the doctor. She ignored me and kept talking about the time I had seen Teresa cure her in the village. Meanwhile she was rubbing or whipping my stomach and cock with a plant that looked like a horsetail. At the same time, I thought she was caressing herself but then I felt her urine along my legs; watched her dumbfounded as she rubbed it onto my stomach, kneading my bladder. The pain was so intense that I fainted, or thought I did, for I was in a deep sleep, screaming.

And yet I heard her singing to me. There was also steam all around the room, and faintly I heard sounds like water boiling and found it relaxing to hear the bubbling which took on its own peculiar rhythm, a drum to which Tsari tuned her singing. It was completely dark, and I kept telling myself that water does not boil without fire.

"I know you can't be here," I said to that shape kneeling over me.

"Didn't you call to me? I heard your voice. I was very far away and it took a long time to get here. Now, you must listen to me: You encounter a lust of darkness, you are soiled, in the supreme belly are you, you are held by a great causer of pain. I lay my hands on the poison. The seat of my incantation is my dark furrow. I call the poison, the black clotted blood. I call the eruptions of fire. Shortly ago, you caused the fire inside. I will charm you. With me comes the white water lily. Take the coolness of my hand. I wish to break the spell. I will let it go back into the earth, back into the hot moist swampy places."

Because her words made sense to me, I thought I was delirious. But the pain had eased. I tried to reach out for her.

"Lie down," she said, "I felt something would happen to you. I have been praying that it wouldn't and yet you do what you should without being told. I have to be curious about you, you were able to call me with your pain."

I tried to speak but whenever I thought of anything to say, it made no sense. My mouth was dry and I was glad when she gave me some of the hot water to drink. It tasted like a fresh tea, made from greens. Then I realized I could not stand any more water in my system. It was very dark for some time, and then I was drinking more of whatever was in the cup. The more hot tea I drank the cooler I became. I felt as if the window were open, a cool winter breeze enveloping me.

More and more I came to realize that I was in a swamp, and that it was rank, that everything was rotting and had become stagnant. There was fire in my belly and I was sure I had been tied over hot coals, and they were slowly burning through me. I expected to get up and find a big black hole in my stomach. I refused to awaken to this reality. My arms and legs were somehow wrapped in a tight cloth which prevented me from moving. I struggled and finally called to Tsari to let me loose.

I was too numb to turn over and kept staring at a beam of light glued to the floor. It led to the bed and I wondered what I was doing on the floor. Then I was awake. The blanket was soaked with my urine, the intense pain was gone, and so was Tsari. I felt a cold breeze and got up to close the window; the room was exactly as Brito had left it.

I went for a leisurely walk around the hacienda, admiring the greenness of the small oak trees which seemed so strange on a landscape of winter branches. When I returned to my room the doctor and Brito were waiting for me.

"It's a long ride out here," the doctor complained as I walked in.

"I'm sure I had cystitis," I said, forgetting that the pain was nearly gone.

"You couldn't have," he answered.

"Ask Brito. I thought a rock had pierced my groin."

"Cystitis doesn't vanish, and without medication there is not much chance of getting rid of the pain so quickly. And to think I was up all night delivering a baby."

"I feel fine," I said sheepishly.

"Then you were never sick with what you claim. Perhaps I should examine you for syphilis; you know the symptoms come and go."

"That's not necessary," I said emphatically. I then thanked him for coming and watched him berating Brito as he walked out of the courtyard. I went to the back window and found where I'd left the blanket. I gathered dead branches and started them burning. I was a bit confused, but as I put the blanket in the flames I knew that was what she wanted me to do. The smoke settled above the fire for a while, then drifted off, turning bluish and disappearing in the haze of the mountains.

Fifteen

Somewhere there was an explanation for my cure. I didn't know exactly where to look or to go, and there were more everyday events which occupied me. I couldn't concentrate solely on the other side with all its warnings and impossible connections. It was too much like examining entrails, and I was expected to produce results no matter what the omens were.

Finally there was the day that Brito freed himself from the winter snarls at the ranch and said that he had to go to the village because it would soon be spring. I had been waiting weeks for him; each day he was almost ready to go. I'd been trying to foresee a future with Tsari but even the roads leading to the village were blocked because of heavy snowfalls in the mountains.

"Do you think Tsari's people will move soon?" I asked him.

"I don't think they will have any other choice. You still don't trust me, my friend, but it is clear to me that it will happen as I have said."

"Why, Brito? Or are you holding out on me again?"

"You must learn to wait and see, for even I don't know why it will happen by spring; it is a feeling again."

"Whatever happens," I said, "I don't want it to interfere with Tsari and me. We should not be dependent on what happens to the whole village."

"You cannot separate her from the village. I know this bothers you, as does the old woman, for she keeps Tsari in the mountains. You must think we are all crazy, no?"

"The stranger she is, the more I find myself loving her, but it's hard to get used to her powers, or whatever you want to call them."

"You are finding out about their traditional ways. We will have to wait and see what happens."

"We can each play for our own stakes."

"I suppose that is so. You are no longer a wild card. You have your own plans."

We barely made it through the main pass, after digging ourselves out of the drifts several times. I was in a hurry to see Tsari, and at the same time I felt closer to Brito. But it was a different relationship. We had our own dreams to fulfill, and understanding each other created a friendly rivalry. If the Opatas didn't move, I would be out of a job—that was clear. But what I wanted most was Tsari.

Brito went to speak with her uncle, and I went looking for her. Her father told me that she had waited for me but then had gone off with Teresa the day before, and he didn't know when they would be back. I was visibly upset and he tried to cheer me up. I wanted to wait for her, but having brought Brito along meant that I would have to go back with him. I was angry at him even though it wasn't his fault. But he had delayed me, and I knew that the more I tied myself to his problems, the more difficult it would be to see Tsari.

While making some minor repairs on the jeep, I saw Brito and the headman talking intently as they walked toward the abandoned church. The church was used as a source of building materials and was surrounded by debris. It would have been good to know what they were saying, but I promised myself to keep out of it. I wondered if the old man knew that Brito felt the village could no longer survive.

The two men disappeared into the rubble of the church, and I forgot about them when I saw a government pickup truck stop in front of Tsari's father's home. Two uniformed police leapt out and went inside carrying their rifles. I hoped Silvera was not still inside, but they came out with him. It was bitterly cold and he had no jacket on; his hands were cuffed behind his back. The Rurales fired several shots in the air, and this brought a crowd into the road.

Silvera was forced to get into the back of the pickup,

while the two uniformed men leveled their rifles at the crowd. The younger one said, "We are going to take your headman with us to the town. It would be foolish for any of you to try and stop us."

Everyone was bewildered. The Rurales had mistaken Silvera for his brother and were unaware of their mistake.

"What do you want?" one of the women shouted in a derisive voice.

"We do not want any trouble," the other man said, "and so we will keep your headman in a safe place. Some of your men have not returned to the mine, and they have not returned the dynamite they accidentally took from the mine when they left. You know who they are. You know that when you have returned all the dynamite, your headman will be allowed to return."

"We are just doing our job," his companion yelled.

Everyone was puzzled until a voice said, "My people, we have a very meager life. Each of us knows that it is an injustice to accuse our young men. We cannot be called criminals. It is a long way between here and the town."

He finished speaking when I thought he was just getting started. It was the old man. Brito now stepped to the front of the crowd. The Rurales were surprised to see him. They asked him what he was doing here. He replied that he was visiting relatives. The two men looked alarmed, and quickly got into their truck.

It was their bad luck that the truck would not start right away. And by the time the engine turned over, they were surrounded by women. They shouted at the women and they cursed; then they started rolling the truck into the group to see if they were actually going to bar the way. The women stayed, but it made no sense, for the truck would eventually ease its way through them. I should have kept my eye on the Indians who had quietly disappeared. Soon, in desperation, the younger man leaned out the door and fired one shot at the ground. A woman screamed in pain. It was a foolish move on his part, but it was already too late. The last thing he must have seen was that chief he thought they had in the back, standing in front of the truck. The Indians aimed their rifles at the windshield. All the shots echoed simultaneously. The truck's engine continued racing in neutral.

The wounded woman was taken into the house and Silvera was helped out of the truck and untied. Most of the people stood staring at the truck, but not bothering to go near it. I was still startled and all I could think about was how they would get away with killing two Rurales, and letting the exhaust smoke steam in the frosty air, for no one went to shut the engine off.

"It is finished here," I said to Brito when he came out.

"I don't think it is that time, yet," he answered coldly.

"The police have every excuse they need to close down the village."

"Why's that?"

"Damn it, Brito, two men were just killed here. I thought you wanted your people to be safe."

"It happens all the time in the winter," he said. "A truck goes off a curve and falls into a part of the barranca that no one can get into until spring. You yourself know that the roads are very dangerous at this time of the year."

"You know that once this kind of violence gets started no one will be safe up here."

"Then we had better get back ourselves."

"I'd rather wait for Tsari," I said angrily.

"No," he said. "You still work for me, I think, and we have a lot to do."

"We can change that situation right now," I said, but before I was able to finish my thought, he began to smile. His smile eased the tension, and the truck finally stalled, initiating a new silence.

"Ay, amigo," he said, "it is not so simple, hey?"

Sixteen

"There is a hidden plan to our lives," Tsari came to tell me. "That is why we never got to the sacred place before; that is why there was a rockslide on the way." She said this with absolute seriousness and there was no doubt in my mind that she meant it.

"The reason we never got there," she continued, "is because you thought you could do whatever you wanted. Once you thought you could come and go as you please. Now you know that you must wait for me. If we had gone to the 'stones' then, you would have only laughed and thought they were odd. But they are very old, and if we go now, then you will see that you too must find the hidden plan in them."

"I am willing to go with you," I said, "because I still would like to know what makes any place sacred."

"It is because it is an entrance to the other side."

"But what makes it an entrance?"

"It is different for everyone, I suppose. But the *komales* are what you must see because the difficulties you have in understanding are still a great barrier between us. I don't know what you've learned, for you are still always asking questions."

"I learned not to trust the canyon."

"It will be different this time."

I can't explain how she decided we could make it up the ledge this time, for my previous attempt remained a vivid memory. I saw it again and again at night while I tried to sleep peacefully. Perhaps this is why I found the ledge almost familiar and was almost able to enjoy the ordeal of traversing it. There was beauty in the adventure of it. Tsari would have claimed the canyon was simply being kind to us, as she predicted.

I was uncomfortable with the idea that life could follow predictions. To conceive of such a possibility I tried to remember those concepts in science where only nonlinear time accurately graphed events. I equated this with going back and forth in my memory but it never seemed real. She could not discuss it, and claimed I was looking in the wrong direction: for explanations rather than signs. She would imply that I was ready to love her before we ever met on the hill. She had this uncanny knack for finding an effect before every cause.

Around the bend in the canyon, the one we had not gotten

beyond, was a high waterfall, and beneath it a small island in the shape of a pyramid. There was nothing unnatural about it. The equal dispersion of the water as it tumbled over the cliff above had honed the rock to one of nature's basic shapes. The particular red-gold color of the canyon was the residue of the soil washed down from the mountains which formed the good farming land below. Since the snows were melting, the falls ran and shrouded the island in a fine mist. We were in the large amphitheater carved by the water as it circled the island. There was an aura of sanctity about the place because it was beautiful and untouched.

The full thrust of the falls fell short of the island, and where the water divided it was shallow enough to cross over. The smoothness of the rock made me question the feasibility of trying to climb to the top. But the ancient handiwork of man made it possible, a stairway cut into the rock, which lent to the atmosphere of a sacred place. As we ascended, I discovered that the top was not as pointed as it had appeared; rather it was a platform with a shallow crater inside. She didn't know who made the stairway or who had set the *komales* into the rim of the well.

There were indeed a set of round flat stones lining the rim, which was about ten feet wide. On them were chiseled white lines, stick-figures like a child might make, and they resembled cuneiform writing. There were men and animals and celestial shapes in a variety of combinations, each stone having only one drawing upon it. I'd heard that similar pictographs had been found in the Bavispe Barranca, but they came from an ancient time and no one knew much about them. It was obvious that this pyramid in the center of the canyon had excited people even in remote times, but I didn't see anything more than pictures on the rocks themselves.

"When you know how to ask yourself to," she told me, "you can concentrate on these figures until they tell you what to do. They reveal themselves, for the carver has put his spirit into them."

"Are they sacred because they are old, is that it?"

"No, no, it is because they are alive, and like a calendar of days they reach their time each year."

As she spoke, I suspected that her people had used these stones for meditation, perhaps taking some drug to help them to visions. The very antiquity of the carvings would have special significance, could arouse superstition. I felt that these carvings helped the Indians of this region maintain their tradition. Yet they stood between Tsari and me more than any other language barrier. I knew what they were historically and that she shouldn't hold them in reverence. She could explain how they were used but not what they meant, yet she was sure they had meanings which could be intuited. I was more impressed by the view of the canyon from this point, the white turbulence of the water as it swirled along the boulders two thousand feet below the tree-lined edge above.

I finally got Tsari to admit that the glyphs had no definite meaning. "They are not words," she said, "and that is why you can't make them talk. They are experiences. I wonder if I should have ever brought you here. How can you look and not feel what they tell you?" The glyphs were arranged in rows which followed the circle of the cone and there was no beginning or end. "Look at the man with his arms bound to a tree, and at this one where the sun and moon face each other."

It was late in the afternoon, and just that time of day when the sun began to set behind the canyon wall, and in the east the moon emerged, a pale white outline above the opposite ledge. They seemed to hang suspended in equal balance, one waxing as the other waned. And of course she would have known this, known that it was the right time of year and that when she pointed out the picture to me, I would see it come to pass. And it made sense that someone in this spot long ago would have seen fit to represent this odd phenomenon, to carve it into rock. She had carefully brought me here at just the right instant to impress me with the magic of the glyphs, and she appeared delighted, assured that her trick had worked.

She caught me looking at her and turned away, facing toward the winding expanse of the canyon while the wind blew through her hair. The scene was lovely even if she had staged it and yet it was frightening to be part of a moment that was ageless, as if there was no reason for the cosmic regularity, other than to reach the same still point that banished the distinction between the past and the present. And while I was discovering something old and she was laughing to herself, it occurred to me that it was not only she who had planned this. Whoever had drawn this scene on the rock had meant others to find it, and to know that he too had been awed by the balance of the sun and moon. I was delighting in this fact, this constancy of the human spirit, when as one sensation led to another and I started mentally jumping around, it became obvious that I was standing outside of the cosmic regularity. The day could move forward into night or back into morning. And as long as the moment lasted, the choice was mine—I could have crossed to the other side right then.

Seventeen

When the spring thaw began, I went to the village planning to stay for several days. I didn't know that Tsari was waiting for Teresa to come and get her or that she felt I had failed her at the *komales*. Since I had last been to the village, there was a new and uncomfortable tension. Everyone was on edge about the Rurales, and there was no indication that anyone planned to move. Rather, I felt a sense of suicidal desperateness—one exemplified by the headman's behavior, for he was talking about the days of the revolution when no dam existed and no strangers were safe in the mountains. The mood was at odds with the bright spring colors, and there was little joy.

Once Teresa came, she quickly confronted the old chief who had been drinking heavily. A few people were watching but Teresa was in such a rage that her voice carried throughout the village.

"You are lost," she screamed. "You don't know whether it is day or night. You have been gnawing the trunks of old trees. If the very circle of the sky were on fire, you wouldn't have the sense to go hide. Let the diviners guard the crossing from the here to the hereafter. You are lucky I don't burn your house down and set your feet on fire."

The old man had been taken by surprise, and now he just tried to get a firm foothold on the ground, while wagging his head and blinking as if to draw a bead on her. She would not come easily into focus, for she was all howls and gyrations.

"You can't even stand up. What am I to think of you? Go ahead, paint the edges of the sun red with whiskey. Take your heart and throw it on the ground, cut it into pieces, let everyone step on it. Or go live in the trees like a wild beast. Jump around, roar, make fun. I can hear your bones scraping against each other. You say you are not afraid. Look at you, you have been rotting your head for so many days that you can't find your own way home. I can't tell if you are dead or alive; all I can do is smell you way off in the mountains."

There was no telling what had brought on this fury, and yet there was no stopping it. Perhaps she was trying to cure the old man of his folly.

"How do you know what will happen? Do you just lie

on the ground like a beaten dog and see the future? If you are not a chief, what are you?"

"I judge by what I see," the headman said, trying to regain his composure and at the same time swatting angrily at her words as if they were flies.

"Then I will get a stick and a cane for you," she continued, thrusting herself upon him, "because you are blind. You know what will happen, eh? You will get everyone killed. By then it is too late. What do you think of that? You will never reach eighty, and I will dig up your bones and throw away your hair."

The old man gathered himself together and raised his hand above his head to get attention. But for some reason he could not command the words. All he could say was, "Once . . . once . . . once."

"You should look down at the ground when speaking nonsense," Teresa said to him, and despite her age, she dominated him. She had all her anger, her jaw was now firmly set; and dressed in black, a dark complexion and white shocks of hair, she looked the sorcerer. "I have had bad dreams," she screamed. "I can hardly sleep in the night. I see men running through the trees. Fire flames on the tips of their hands. I hear rumors from the animals I meet in the woods. This is not all I have to say."

Everyone maintained a resolute distance, except for a small boy who chased after his dog, and his dog ran to the confrontation, barking in a futile small-dog way. Teresa turned away, sweeping her skirts so that they would not touch the ground. The old man hollered after her but his words were lost in the barking.

Tsari was smiling, and so I smiled, although I did not know what was amusing. Mostly, the men and women were silent and expressionless, as if whatever had happened was no concern of theirs. Teresa walked among us stamping her feet, looking wildly from one direction to another.

"Look at this one here," she began, and grasped my hands in hers, and by the will of those hands I was separated from everyone. "Look at his eyes. We have been here a long time; I have not felt eyes like these. They have seen into the passageway to the other side; they have seen the light of the stones. He is not even one of us and he sees what you do not know yet. I am an old woman, and soon I will go into the mountains forever. Where will you all be then? Hey?"

She paused to look around. I was totally aware of what she was saying, for the pitch of her voice had taken hold of me, so that I was sure that I was standing in a shower of light. There was no ground, only a vibrato effect, and I felt very warm. Her hands had displaced mine so that I had no sense of touching her. I was partially aware that there were tears in her eyes, and in the silence I could hear the song she was singing to herself, the melody which led into the words. A resonance filled the dome of the sky.

"You want to know where you fit in, don't you?" she asked quietly.

"I do," I heard myself say.

"Is your life still your own?" she said. "Or have you lost your home by coming here?"

"I've found an older home," I said as she let me loose.

"Do you know where you are?"

"Where the great cloud was seen," I said and waved at the sky to mime her.

"He follows his hands," she screamed. "I will show you." She held her hands before my eyes as if trying to show that I could not see too well. We held this ungainly pose for several seconds and I couldn't tell what the others were doing, for her hands blocked out even the sunlight. "You know nothing," she said to me in a quiet voice, "and even knowing is not understanding. Yet your intuitions will come at the touch of your hands. You will take what you need."

"I want to take Tsari," I said.

"You will pay my price first, or I will not let you go."

My eyes started to hurt, a semiblindness, for she had another one of her potions on the palms of her hands which burned like raw onions. If there was a reason for this absurd sorcery I had no idea what to make of it, or what the payment had to be, and I cried out that my eyes were burning.

She pulled her hands away from me, and loudly clapped them in the air. She was now laughing while I stood helplessly in front of the villagers not knowing if I had been made a fool of, or somehow appointed to a mission I had not volunteered for. It was difficult to see because of the tears, but I could hear that others were laughing with her.

"Because he is here," she yelled, "I will give him a gift. Because he must learn to live all over again, I will give him something so that he will not be empty-handed." She reached down and pulled a plant out of the earth, making sure that she had it by the roots. She then stuffed it into my hands.

"With this you can fill the belly, and with this," she chuckled, "you may even be able to make a woman happy." These words brought a roar of laughter.

I started to throw the plant down, but she held my arm back, now smiling, almost affectionate. If she wanted me to hold the roots I would do just that; I had nothing to lose. So I held the plant aloft while she quietly chanted, "Can you, can you put it together? Can you learn it? Can you, white man, can you do it?"

Eighteen

For several days Tsari sat in the sunlight in the courtyard and worked away with her knife on a five-foot branch, using her belly as a platform. The branch was from a blue canela she had brought down from the mountains with her when she left the village to come and live at the ranch. It was now the most important thing in her life and she devoted her full attention to it. Several more days went by before I realized that she was making a bow.

"What is it for?" I asked her when I brought the inner parts of a deer shot by one of the ranch hands, which she had demanded.

"It is for hunting the *tash-chukudd.*"

What she said didn't refer to anything I had ever heard of, but after listening to the dialect spoken at the village I could at least translate it. She said she was going to hunt a day- or sun-owl.

"That sounds like a fine idea," I said. "Where are you going to hunt such a thing?"

"Right here. It is that time of year, and you have already seen one, remember, drawn on the *komales*."

"Yes, I did see an owl drawn on a picture of the sun."

"Well, I now need some narrow yucca stalks and the tips of the cat-claw bush so we shall have the kind of arrows that can't be removed."

"Is that what you need to shoot at this?"

"It is what Teresa uses."

I was beginning to get a sense of what this was all about. She'd said she left the village because she'd had a dream it was not a good place to have the baby. I accepted this at face value, but now I realized that she was frightened. She was unsure about the birth, and it could also have been that Teresa had somehow warned her. At least she was not so expert at seeing into the other side that she had conquered all her fears. I supposed that her desire to hunt an impossible creature came from the comfort that she might receive from any ritual act, like the bow-making.

Oddly enough the time for hunting the sun-owl was just after a thunderstorm when the mist settled on the ground. I had been drinking late with Brito, but nevertheless she woke me early to say that the shower I didn't know had occurred was over and that it was time to go. She had finished the deer-gut string while supposedly I was wasting my time talking.

"Don't look so serious," she said as I grudgingly began to dress. "The other side is riddled with places for laughter."

I tried to ignore my hangover and look cheerful so that she would feel I was deeply involved. It was the way I had to comfort her, to support her, for it was often a difficult pregnancy and this in itself surprised me since she was such a strong woman.

We had to go into the arroyo where the trees grew tallest, and it had not crossed my mind that she was searching for a suitable spot for when the time came. The sun had cleared the mountains. There was a lush green smell and every plant was on the verge of blooming, and yet it was impossible to examine anything closely with the settling ground fog. The riverbed narrowed as we got beyond sight of the ranch and we walked a long time, trying to keep from being impaled on the long spines that protected each plant we stepped through, and the only sound was that of rattlesnakes which coiled and warned us as we passed by.

"I would like to talk about this some more," I said after we reached a place where the river bottom became mired with an amber clay that had a moist, spongy texture, which made every step a labor.

"From here on," she said, "we will have to be quiet." She picked out two arrows and began rubbing them together as we walked on. I followed her determination more than anything else, for I knew that each step had to be hard on her belly and back. Frequently, we startled the kangaroo rats, which explained why there were so many snakes hunting around us. But I did not see anything else and the fog held the sun's glare like a mirror, forcing me to blink to keep my eyes adjusted. We were inside a rainbow and the prismatic colors tinted the misty air.

After I bumped into her and she yelled at me for being careless, I asked: "How the hell are we going to see in this?" But she was already into that world of her own. She had placed an arrow into the bow and was testing the spring and the tension. It was quite ludicrous to watch her trying to keep the bow away from her breasts and protruding belly. I thought she would let me try it too.

"This is my branch for looking to the other side, and if you want one, you will have to make your own. It's carved just for my hand and for my eye. You cannot eat a *tash-chukudd* but the wings of one will make the future clearer, like giving vision to those who are blind."

I saw nothing where she was aiming but a small knoll bathed in a dazzling light just where the arroyo turned and dropped down into a ravine. There were trees on top but the glare was too great to make anything else out. Tsari was totally absorbed in aiming at the top of the knoll. She didn't draw the arrow but rather sighted down its shaft, using the bow and arrow as one might use a water-witching stick. The tip of the arrow may even have wavered in response to some aspect of the dampness. She held the bow awkwardly and I was surprised to notice something she did ungracefully. After staring in the direction she was aiming, I finally saw a blurred brown spot at the base of the trees, more like a hole in the fog than any animal shape.

When she drew back the arrow, her whole body became focused on that spot, and not a muscle moved or shook as she set the arrow in flight. We watched it disappear into the fog, or I did, for she was already about to release the second one. Again, she was searching for something at a point just beyond our sight. Her release was smoother, as she stood with her knees bent, feet flat, and shoulders turned toward the target. This time I thought I heard the arrow strike a stone somewhere on the hill.

"Almost," she cried. "Can you see?"

The last phrase was said in such an excited high-pitched voice that I had an uncomfortable flashback. It was Teresa's voice, an exact duplication. Its sound gave rise to a prickly sensation of heat and I had to get off my feet, to sit down to keep from entering the vertigo. The tunnel in the fog was now similar to the shaft through which I had seen Tsari on the ledge, and it was not exactly some mythical bird I saw. The brown oval in the fog took on the glow of the sun, of Teresa's healing fire, and I saw what I should have seen along time ago: it was Teresa and Tsari fused together and synchronized, and the strength passing from Teresa's body into hers. It had been an act, one whose existence I had not heard of, where the power, the abilities were being transferred so that they might be passed on. I was alarmed at what this had to mean for our relationship. Tsari not only believed she had crossed over, but that she was to become a healer, and inherit the work of a *curandera.*

Whether this was tradition or belief, or the true passing of some mystical healing skill, it was not something that delighted me, for I thought I would eventually lose her to that reality behind the one in which we loved each other. I had never seen it quite so well before. There was no chance of rationally choosing the course of our lives if she believed she had taken on the *curandera's* responsibilities. The present suddenly took on a one-dimensional aspect which made me so sad that I felt like weeping.

I was brooding all the time I followed her to the knoll and it was only fitting that she never noticed or paid any attention. She asked me to look for her arrows and I agreed because I wanted to be away from her. I searched all through the underbrush, while thinking that she might leave suddenly unless some unexpected change occurred in both of us. The arrows, made of the same materials as the brush, were impossible to locate.

"Your arrows are lost," I said.

"No, they are on the other side; I want you to see this for yourself. You could look all day and you would not find them unless you crossed over."

I was tempted to stay and prove to her that the arrows were here. I knew I could find them. Unconsciously, I began scanning the area again to see if I could catch sight of them.

"It doesn't matter," she said. "We can go home now. I was only practicing, for there is much concentrating to be done when the time comes. You know, I just felt the baby kicking again."

Nineteen

It was impossible for Tsari and me to discuss rationally the customs of coming and going. I was so used to having people tell me when they were leaving, where they were going, and when they were coming back, that her habit of taking off when she pleased was emotionally draining. I had promised not to be upset about this form of independence, but still I tried to get her to be more considerate. She felt that she was called from one place to another and that waiting to tell me where she was going made it impossible to follow her inner voices. I tried to encourage her to change by always mentioning what I was going to do. She would shake her head in wonder; plans were foolish, she said, because life changes from day to day.

I overslept one morning, and woke to find everyone at the

ranch packing up as if to go on a holiday. Then I was told that they were going to the river since it was flowing for the first time in two years. That's impossible, I thought.

"It is flowing," they said.

I went looking for Tsari only to find out that she had already left the ranch with some of the vaqueros. There was only one possible explanation for why the river was flowing, and I was afraid that she would have deduced this and gone first to the river and then up to the dam itself to see what had happened. I was just as alarmed as she must have been, but could not believe she would attempt such a trip at the risk of the child. I didn't have much time to think about it, for Brito's truck roared in through the main gate. I went to meet him and saw that he was alarmed, suppressing a frantic energy.

"You will have to help me," he said.

"What happened?" I wanted to know. "I hear the river is running."

"The dam gave way," he said, "and the Rurales will believe the Opatas dynamited it. It is the simplest thing to believe, otherwise they must admit that the *mordida* ate up some of the building money. I have known for some time that the dam was not of the best construction."

"If they believe the Opatas stole the dynamite from the mine, they will have both Mexicans and Americans after them," I said.

"They will have everyone after them, but the dynamite was not for the dam; it was for the pass. He wanted his mountain retreat, for there are no Indian reservations in Mexico. If he now decides to seal the dam off, he may be safe, but there will be a lot of people in serious trouble, so we cannot just stand around here and talk about it as if it were over."

"I think that Tsari has gone up there; and if what you say is true it would be just like her."

"I need you now, for we must do my people a favor and take them as many guns as we have stored here."

"You're serious," I said after taking in the tension in his usually jovial face.

"They will have to defend themselves until they see that the ranch is the safest place. Most will follow Silvera, but even so it will not be easy to move out of the mountains with the pass closed and the Rurales searching for them. I did not know it would happen this way, but I mustn't forget where I belong now."

The day had taken on a complexity which seemed inevitable, except that I didn't know where she was and above all else I wanted to find her. There were too many old hatreds to consider, but I got the general picture as Brito drove the truck up to an old storm cellar behind the garage.

"Let the men help us," I said to him.

"They might talk about it afterwards," he said. "Only you can help me now, for the ranch must remain a neutral place."

If only she had told me where she was going when she left, I repeated over and over as we headed up the familiar road to the mountains. The river was crashing through the canyon with a fury it hadn't had since I arrived. Tsari was not by the road or the area where the peach trees grew, but I had no idea what time she had left the ranch. The river had been flowing all night, Brito said. And though I could see for myself that the abundance of water was more than the melting snows could provide, I had lived so long assuming that the river would never flow from its source again, that it was as if I was traveling in a different country entirely.

I considered what might happen to the village, to the farm, to the people caught between these two places; and yet the future would not come clear. The present itself was bewildering. So, when we reached a vantage point above the river, I expected to see the massive concrete walls of the dam shattered completely.

I didn't expect to see a gathering of people along the rampart that braced it to the canyon; there was only a small crack going down the center of it, as if a lightning bolt had streaked through it. At the very bottom, several floodgates had been ripped away, and from there the water poured out into the canyon.

When we arrived at the dam, I was surprised to see how many people were there. I had never seen most of them; many were Yaqui or Tarahumaura, for all the Indians who lived in the mountains had gathered to watch the dam collapse. "You can't give guns to everyone," I told Brito, hoping that the number of Indians would make him forget his plan.

He agreed that he would have to see what the situation was.

The atmosphere was almost festive. There were many younger men and women, and almost all were drinking *pulque,* a dubious gift of the *agave* plant. We parked the truck among the trees and I told Brito that I would look for Tsari.

"I think we should stay together. It will be safer for you if you are with me."

He explained that any white man would not be safe, and that it would take only a small push to shove someone over the wall. Considering the drunkenness, I decided he was right.

The weather was pleasant and the mood gay, as if they had all come to watch a parade. The men and women dressed in their Sunday clothes, and a good deal of carousing and courting was taking place. The mountains had always appeared so deserted to me that I was surprised at how many people still held on to the old ways. Some people had built fires on the rampart and were beginning to cook their afternoon meal. There was a fine pungent odor of burning mesquite mixed with the sweet liquor smell. A good portion of the men were already drunk, and couples were disappearing into the woods behind them, as was the custom at ceremonies when the normal rules of behavior were ignored. But this was not a ceremony.

The old man must have believed it was, for he was dancing along the embankment and acting like a medicine man working in a movie. "Why, Brito?" I asked.

"Because he thinks his prayers have been answered. I think he feels that he will have the attention of all the young men and women who live up here. He sees himself as a chief from the old days."

Indeed, there was a lot of loose talk about the old days, about keeping everyone but Indians out of the mountains. One man was saying that they could prevent the dam from being repaired. It was hard to believe they could be oblivious to such things as the new Border Cooperation project, but then they didn't read the newspapers. I didn't know what Brito was thinking; the mood around us hinted that anything was possible.

I was watching a group of Opatas and Yaquis who were drinking and eating by one of the fires. I tried to listen to what Brito was telling Silvera but my eyes kept going back to that group. There was something peculiar about one of the women. It finally dawned on me that this woman was wearing the same outfit Tsari had worn when she claimed me at the village, the same purple blouse and long blue skirt. When she turned toward me I was immediately attracted by the resemblance to Tsari.

"Who is that woman?" I asked Silvera.

"*Mi puta,*" he said with disgust, "and she had the same mother as her sister."

"You are sure you haven't seen Tsari?" I asked him for the second time.

He assured me that he hadn't, but I was still nervous

about not being able to find her and decided to question her sister.

The girl—she was taller and more slender than Tsari—seemed to recognize me as I approached, but I knew I had never seen her before. She was hardly ever mentioned.

"Have you seen Tsari up here?" I asked her.

"This is the one whose eyes burn everything in their sight," she said to the group and all began to laugh. I gathered that I had been the subject of a story.

"How come you cannot see for yourself?" a man with long hair asked with a belly laugh.

"She is in the woods," her sister said. "I will take you to where she is."

I followed her back into the pine trees and she said nothing but seemed to be going to a specific place.

"When did you see her?" I asked.

"Not long ago," she said. She wore makeup, which I felt was unusual, and had such a coy manner that I was beginning to suspect she was playing.

"I'm serious," I said.

"So am I," she said and proceeded to draw her tongue across her lips as if she were signaling someone at a bar. I grabbed her by the shoulders and shook her to make her stop, but she only used the movement to weave her body close to me. "My sister says I should find someone like you if I am going to live on the border. What do you think?"

"I am worried about your sister. Don't you care?"

She pulled away from me, saying: "I am younger and prettier."

"You didn't see her here."

"I wouldn't lie."

She looked me straight in the eyes and pouted, and these gestures struck me so deeply that reflexively I slapped her hard across the face, recoiling at the sight of her features and those eyes which could have been those of her sister. She giggled and I wished I'd slapped her harder.

I felt she would cause me some trouble and returned to the truck, but by the time I got to where we'd left it, Brito had moved it, and I was sure that he was giving out the guns we brought. Silvera had probably decided who should have them. I tried to stay out of sight, watching the ramp in case I could locate Brito or Tsari. I now had a clearer head and was not sure that she should have come up here to begin with. I searched among the trees at the edge of the ramp to find the truck, when all of an instant it was completely quiet along the ramp: the odd calm just before a storm hits. I couldn't figure it out and went to see. On the other side of the dam, along the opposite rampart, Teresa was waving her arms and shouting. Her presence itself was a signal to be quiet, and the Indians were trying to catch her words over the roar of the river below. I couldn't hear but there followed a mad scramble to clear the ramps. I jumped when someone touched my shoulder. Brito said, "Take the truck—it is on the road—and get out of here."

"What is it?"

"The Rurales are coming up from the States side. They will cross over the dam itself."

I could imagine how incriminating it must have looked from a Border Patrol helicopter, for instance, to see all these people camped along the dam. It would be assumed that the Indians were celebrating not their luck, but their crime. "Will you stay here?"

"No, we will scatter into the mountains. It will take some time to gather up possessions and reach safety. I will do what I can, but it has nothing to do with you. I will send people to you at the ranch."

"It's not so simple," I said. "I can't leave you here."

"It is my home," he said. "I understand how you feel, but trust me one more time. It is best for me to have you at the ranch."

I didn't want to believe him right away and looked around to decide if everything he said were true. I saw that we were the only people standing still. "We will do it as you say this time," I said, wanting to embrace him. I just stood there, about to promise him I'd take care of things while he stayed here.

"Get going," he yelled.

I remember running and being joined by Opatas who wanted a ride back to the village. As I started the truck I took one last look at the dam. Teresa was nowhere in sight, but the old man was now dancing at the center above the crack, oblivious to everything and stomping up and down as if trying to collapse the dam by his own efforts. He was still dancing when the first shot snapped through the air and we took off.

There wasn't much left of the dirt road which had been built to haul equipment and supplies for the dam, but at each curve I expected to meet a truck filled with police. Everywhere was the wrong place and I drove recklessly as if I were being chased, appreciating the virtues of Brito's special truck. None of the men or women with me complained; this was the way they drove all the time. I hardly watched the road itself but kept peering into the trees and down the slopes looking for Tsari. When we reached the village, I stopped long enough to make sure she wasn't there. Only two men wished to stay with me and they rode in the back.

After we left I drove slower and slower not fully sure what would happen when I reached the pass. I wasn't quite sure that Brito was telling me the truth about the old man's intentions, but when we found the pass buried in a landslide I lost all doubts. Someone had been left behind to attend to this task. There was no way to get the truck through and this explained why we hadn't seen any Rurales. I fully believed that the chief had not planned anything for the dam; he just wanted his old seclusion back, with or without water.

I drove around a little and found a ditch partially hidden by trees and left the truck there. It was the best I could do. The men with me said they were going into the hills down where I first met Tsari. I warned them to stay out of sight and they laughed, actually laughed as if this were the way it was meant to be. We laboriously picked our way across the boulders strewn across the pass, alert to the possibility that the Rurales might be waiting below. I felt there would be this kind of terror in the mountains until some miracle could resolve the deep hatred between Indians and the government. There was no one in sight as we climbed down the other side of the pass and went our separate ways. Once I was alone, the situation seemed more desperate, and I didn't know who I wouldn't see alive again.

In the peach grove along the river I could see the men and women from the ranch swimming and picnicking, oblivious to what had happened. I wasn't close enough to see faces but I prayed that Tsari would be with them. It was almost dusk and I was aware that I had to hurry if I were to catch a ride back to the ranch. I ran, trying to maintain a pace that would not exhaust me, for the direct path was along the sandy bank where each stride was difficult.

I almost stumbled on her. She was sitting in the shade of an enormous cottonwood, resting among its roots and eating freshwater crayfish raw from the river. And this, too, suddenly struck me as inevitable, as if I should have known all along. So I could hardly be angry at her.

Twenty

Soon, groups of women came down to the ranch using old trails that were still safe, and they told us various stories about what was happening in the mountains. The rumor was that the old man was dead, but some said he was living with others up in the highest ranges. From what I heard, I assumed that the Rurales were under orders to guard the dam and drive the Indians out of the mountains once and for all. Day by day I was learning of their tactics and it didn't ease my mind. We had no word from Brito, Teresa, or Silvera. Tsari's problems with her pregnancy had to take second place as I struggled to manage the ranch and find living quarters and supplies for those already moving down. Luckily, the weather was good and people could live outside.

I went to bed exhausted and did not look forward to waking up.

One night while lying in bed, I mentioned to Tsari that I had seen her sister and was not impressed. She made me tell her everything that happened.

"I am not caring about what you did to her; I want to know who she was with."

"With Yaquis, I think."

"Then you must drive me to the church in Magdalena on this Sunday. It is time for her to take care of my father. So I must speak to her, and that is where she will be."

"You know I can't leave the ranch now, and from what I saw I don't think that speaking to her will do any good."

"Then I will go myself."

She was not to be dissuaded, and her mood was not too good with all the talk of violence in the mountains, and the village's fate uncertain. So on the Saturday before Easter we left for this town, a good distance away. We took Brito's sedan because she felt a jeep would be too rough on her.

We arrived late at night and slept in the car. In the morning when I saw how many people had invaded the small town, and what a celebration was in progress, I felt we were on fool's errand. There would be no way to find her sister if she were actually here. There were many Indians from all over Sonora and Sinaloa, and in the fiesta mood it was the children who dominated. I saw mothers nursing the infants they carried in serape slings, and babies carried by toddling brothers and sisters, a total profusion of these wildflowers, as if faith meant conception. I felt surrounded by women who were with child. It was a bazaar of big bellies and Tsari fit right in, displaying herself. We could hardly walk without becoming entangled in the swarm of children leading each other around by the hand. They got into the displays of goods on the sidewalks around the plaza, and played under the trucks of the hawkers whose mad loudspeakers blared bargains. They were on and under the tables of the food-mongers whose eating cribs broke the crowd into those who favored fish or fowl, beef or pork. They slid along the cars, around the benches, and among the trees, where the parents alternately prayed and drank themselves faithless.

The townspeople had become the onlookers and they kept a passive eye on the Indians. It seemed that lawlessness was forgiven, and the Son of God was about to rise into heaven, heralded by the ringing of the church bells in the two towers that framed the hill behind the town. In the very center of things were the herb sellers, other Indian women down from the mountains wearing their long festive camp dresses. Before them they had innumerable small packets containing barks and leaves, weeds and flowers. As we neared the church, there were more children, the older ones dressed in paper Franciscans' robes and waiting their turn to go in.

On the steps were many beggars seeking alms with a beautiful wretchedness, the women displaying their babies at the breast and holding out their free hands, and the maimed men, the infirm and the blind, waiting for charity with tin cans. The great carved wood doors were swung open to let air and light into the stone sanctuary, and inside I saw the black figures of those kneeling in the rows of wooden pews below the people standing in the aisles and along the walls beneath the chipped and peeling murals of saints in purple robes beneath azure skies. In the vestibule there was another crowd milling around the wooden effigy of the patron Saint Francis which was wrapped in white linen and pinned with silver charms, the *talismanes* of those beseeching a favor. We moved through a weaving of arms reaching to the cloth for a touch or a kiss. A breeze passing through open arches brushed us as we passed between the milling figures, testing the flame of the candles whose gentle smoke stained the angels suspended on the walls to guard the sanctuary.

And in the center of the cruciform church, above the stone altar, there was an undistinguished little man, whose arms beseeched the figure on the great cross above him, and whose eyes focused on the statue of the Virgin Mary while all heads were bowed, and his litany was lost among the blaring megaphones outside.

We stood by a grave at the corner of the plaza. The missionary's bones lay within, protected by a stone and glass pavilion. The small bones and tiny skull lay bleached on the brown earth, having been moved here from somewhere else after this long-dead Father Kino was commemorated for christianizing this region of the Pimeria Alta.

"I am sorry we didn't see your sister," I said. "What do you want to do?"

"We must wait until the night-hawks come."

"That doesn't mean anything to me."

"I think she is one of them; her spirit is like theirs. You have seen those small hawks which flit around the light of the plaza at night. Don't you remember what I was doing when I met you?"

"You were trapping birds."

"Well, I must trap her spirit. I must call it to me and trap it; then she will have to listen to me."

"Do you think you can do it?"

"I will try, for my father's sake and for my sister's sake. I will try to find the voice. If only it were quiet here like it was on the hill."

It seemed so long ago that we had met by chance on that hill. She was not the same woman, for now she was lovely and in bloom. Like other couples, we walked and held hands, but I still did not know how to ask her how she called the birds to that hill. Any words I had led to an answer which could not make sense. It was best to forget about it and go to eat.

Then we talked with Papagos who had walked a hundred miles to be here; we spoke with the Tarahumaras camped along the railroad tracks who came from the south in cattle cars; and with Yaquis who hung around their pickup trucks; and with Seri Indians who had come to town to sell carvings; but we did not see her sister.

When the lamp poles alone kept evening from descending upon the plaza, Tsari decided that she would return to the church. I knew she had been watching the small hawk-shaped birds she had described, which were now darting and swooping around the lights in small groups, chasing insects. Her full attention was concentrated on these birds and I had to guide her among the people. The church was much more crowded than before and it was barely possible to squeeze in. There were several entrances being used and I did not see how we could locate anyone in this situation. The women wore shawls and it was hard to see faces now that it was dark. The interior lights were set high on the vaulted ceiling and succeeded only in casting shadows below.

There was still a circle of Indians around the bier of the patron saint and we managed to join them, finally pushing our way into the line. Very slowly the line circled around the table. The purpose, I discovered, was to reach the head of the effigy, and once there, to cross oneself, say a prayer lasting seconds or minutes, and then to reach down and lift the head of the effigy from the table, and then to make room for the next person. It went slowly, and yet the mood was not impatient, but the pressure of bodies was urgent compared to the serene expression carved on the face of the saint.

Tsari kept letting people pass us by and I supposed she expected her sister to come here and perform this ritual. "But why would she wish to do this?" I asked. "You do not have a church at the village."

"The people come here to test themselves by lifting the statue's head. If their prayer is not spoken truly, they say the head will not rise, as if it were made of heavy stone. Yet my sister would come here and laugh at how easily the head will lift no matter what she has done."

"Then she comes here for nothing?"

"No, she comes here for this easy forgiveness, something very important to her. That is why I can find her here and I will not forgive, but maybe I will trap her."

The pressure of bodies and voices pushed us toward the front of the bier. There was no simple way to back out and I saw that Tsari was nervous, that her whole body was tense. One man was between us and the statue, and he was mumbling something that sounded like an *Ave Maria*. When Tsari exchanged places with him she put her hands over the eyes of the saint, and began to speak softly:

"We keep the old songs
made of the wind
in our mountains
you cannot see
the scream on the wind
or the wing
that sings in the blood
the breath
that wakens
or hear the word
of the priest
the beggars it makes
the figures of wood

the figures of clay
will not fly
or soar on our wind
to capture the spirit
to cry in its voice
come to the breath
that fathered you
come to the dream
night opens to you
out of the depths
of your own night
the wind is beautiful
alone and listening
all that is past
all that will be
passes lightly
across the land
and lingers forever
come alone
as the bird flies
as the bird hears
to the whistle
come home
come home
no spirit
will pass the crowd
at the door
the crowd

the doors
of wind."

And as she moved away, she was singing to herself, a
wind song, perhaps, in some ancient language whose con-
sonants were like vowels and whose vowels were like conso-
nants. And the sound rose up from her belly, making a sweet
music like the flute to fill the church so that people turned
to touch her as we passed by them until the silence of the
church was interrupted only by the night breeze. But I think
I noticed what no one else saw: that there was one night-
hawk, trapped in the dome, which fluttered helplessly, confused by its own shadow, unable to find the window it had
entered through.

I was hardly aware of how it was done, a poor witness to
the strength behind the incantation; but in it she spoke
directly to the spirit, saying in a few words all it took hours
to say when we did find her sister.

Twenty-One

A small boy, around ten years old, with a badly abscessed tooth, brought me a message that Brito wished to meet me at a wayside inn just beyond the northwestern corner of the ranch. The boy could hardly speak, and hadn't eaten or slept for several days, but I gathered that Brito would be walking out of the mountains. I sent the boy to Tsari and left immediately; it wasn't exactly clear when I was to meet Brito—that night or the night before.

The roads to the border area were hardly more than cattle trails, and since the kind of driving I had to do would burn a lot of gas I filled both tanks and carried two five-gallon cans for good measure. I was driving toward a badly eroded area off the slope of the mountains which looked like a series of giant beehives carved in sandstone.

The vegetation dwindled to a few dry cholla cactus whose squidlike tentacles wavered above a barren clay soil studded with large rocks. I made between ten and twenty miles an hour all afternoon, driving by the compass until I reached something that resembled a road. It came out of the back side of the mountains behind the dam and seemed to lead nowhere. At this junction I switched over to the left tank and waited for the gauge to register. When it didn't, I discovered the tank was punctured and the last of ten gallons was dripping from a jagged hole. I filled the other tank with the cans and went on, aware that I wouldn't have enough gas to get back unless I could buy some.

It was getting dark and there was still no sight of the inn. I drove until I heard a dog barking behind me. It was a dog or a coyote. A dog. I stopped and walked back to where it seemed to be. I couldn't see or hear it anymore and returned to the jeep. I had only five gallons left. I feared that Brito would be waiting for me, and that I would never show up, and no one else would know where I was. Then the dog barked again. I turned around and shined the lights on a live ocotillo fence, which appeared to be part of the terrain but was actually shielding a house. I went inside the yard and found the dog tied to an old station wagon with three tires left on it. The dog was friendly and I didn't see why it had to be restrained.

"Buenas noches," I called out. No light came on but I heard someone stirring inside. Perhaps the dog had already wakened these people, and those in the country were always helpful. The door opened and a man stood looking at me.

"Qué tiene?"

"Nada," I said reflexively. It was nine thirty and I wanted to apologize, but in the dark we could hardly see each other.

"Señor," he said.

"I'm a bit lost," I said. This was explanation enough and he let me in and then lit a candle on a small table by the door. He was a thin old man, light gray moustache and parched lips setting off a drawn, hollow face. I watched him wiggling his bare swollen toes on the earth floor, waiting for me to get the cobwebs of night-driving out of my mind. The candle caught, casting a circle of dim light around us. We were not alone. Several chickens pecked at the floor and their startled clucking was a weird punctuation for our silence. I realized I was in a small bar, and this was the inn, a part of his homestead. I asked him if he had seen anyone else. He hadn't, and I said I could use a drink.

As he left the table I heard someone else moving around in the back and wood being put into a stove. The candles flared on the wire lath and chipped plaster that bandaged the crumbling adobe walls. It was a meager existence. He came back with two cups of coffee and sat down with me, still wearing his long flannel nightshirt. When I mentioned that I had to find some gasoline he said that I wouldn't have any luck, and smiled at me as I grimaced at the bitter strength of his coffee.

"I could pay well for a few gallons," I said, intimating that

I suspected he must have some to get around, for his supplies had to come from somewhere.

"Gas is more scarce than money," he said, "and there is not much money here either."

This casual but pointed remark convinced me that the man had a tank with gas. I just didn't know what he would require to let me buy some. He obviously saved what gas he hauled by himself for emergencies.

"I could return the gas in two days," I said.

"It is a long way from anywhere to this place," he said.

There wasn't much sense in going all the way out here to get Brito and then having us both stranded. It was my obligation to have enough gas in the car and I wasn't going to let the man thwart me. I studied him carefully, trying to perceive in the setting of his world just what he wanted. He had never heard of Brito, and didn't know him even after I described him. I told him I was going out to relieve myself and once outside searched around his yard for any sign of a tank. I couldn't find it but still believed it was buried somewhere. I went back in and had another cup of coffee.

I drank the coffee while the man yawned continuously in front of me. It was still like trying to penetrate an opaque veil. I knew it would be useless to plead with the man, and kept racking my brain for the solution. Finally I was reduced to rocking back on my chair and listening to his dog baying at a pack of coyotes somewhere off in the desert. It howled, and a moment later there would be an echo from the wild dogs. My mind was absorbed with thoughts about the special code between all dogs, all animals. It was not a profound thought by itself, but suddenly the connection was there.

I went out to the jeep and deliberately removed the bolts to my spare tire and returned with it to the house. Then he sent me back for my gas cans. After a lot of talk I had finally made contact.

It was early in the morning when Brito arrived and I just happened to see him walking out of the dawn among the rock and cactus, since the roosters were crowing on the hood of the jeep. His hair was tied back in a ponytail, and he had no shirt on, just a Rurale jacket. He must have been walking all night, for his steps did not quite follow each other, and he wavered slightly along the line between us. I took the canteen and went out to meet him. All the trappings, all the poses were gone; it was the same man I'd first met, but he was like a boy leaving his first home, and on his face were written dreams and plans. The night is a good friend, he had once said. It had left him haggard but stronger.

"My life tells me how limited I am," he said, "how little one man can do, and how far he can go in a short time. We are not far from the border, and yet between the States and here it is not the same world. When I was leaving the mountains, I could look down and see sailboats gliding across the lake—across the 'line.' The water was pouring out from under them, but so slowly they never noticed. I did not intend to come down alone; I hoped Teresa would be with me.

But she will never leave the mountains; no matter how much I pleaded with her she would not come down. She says her time is up, she has lived too long. I told her the garden was finished, that everything was there. It didn't matter, she went on and on about the green tree of abundance; she would go back to the center of souls. And though I had heard it before I could not understand her. She said that you should tell me what she sees. Well, I don't know what it is. You are to work with me, she says, yet I don't even think she knows what you do. But we must finish the dream; there is still no farm, but if the land is good, we will support the people: I have heard it said before, that plants are better than guns.

"But there are some who will not farm, some of the wilder ones and those from the old days of the revolution who love nothing but the mountains. I don't know whether the old man is dead or alive, but more than a few followed him. They went to the old mining camps buried deep in the rocks above the timber line. They say they will fight to keep *los Godammies* from repairing the dam. They will not believe that the past violence belongs with the dead.

"Silvera has gathered all the relatives together; they have nothing left but their names. At least now they agree with each other. They have chosen him to head the new village. It is those who kept the family ties who will be coming down and they bring the traditions. Once they were people of the valleys, and they will find relatives they had forgotten along the Sonora River!

"The dam still holds except for the floodgates, but now they patrol it, and have set up a station with machine guns. All the roads are blocked in one way or another but that will not stop them. They can bring the equipment in by plane, and the dam can be repaired from underwater. It is just a matter of time, so we will take what water comes down to us and hope that the whole structure gives way when the rains are heavy and the graft of the officials comes home to roost. To know what to do with the water, I will rely on you. We will not be the only ranch to begin farming. You will be needed, if you stay.

"What I did was ride and talk to everyone I could, promising them that my land will be like their own—and still I had to promise them cattle. They will all come down when they can, a few at a time at night. We rode and tried to keep out of sight, and shot at the mounted Rurales to keep them away. They killed most of the animals and burned the houses wherever they could. They are either crazy with recklessness or scared, with no in-between. I don't think many people were killed, but it is hard to know, for many lived alone on the high pastures. We went higher, when we really wanted to make our way down. They tried to drive us out of the mountains by cooping us up in their traps, but the time is right now for leaving; the Rurales get tired of the mountains.

"Now I am ready to return with my people, and I'm glad that the boy made it—otherwise you would not be here.

Although he was sick, there was no one to send him with. He is my nephew, Teresa's grandnephew."

"I left him with Tsari," I said. "She said she could take care of his mouth."

"That's good," he said. "You are beginning to understand. It is his faith in her that will help him be well. I was afraid you might have sent him to the clinic, and he would not have survived that."

Twenty-Two

It was not so close to her time that any day the baby might come, and with Brito back things had settled down enough for me to go on a small errand into town. As best I could, I explained to the local pharmacist that I needed a tranquilizer powerful enough to work on a large calf. I actually needed enough for ten such animals because they had broken into Brito's garden, and Tsari had discovered them racing madly through the canyon when she went to tend the plants. They were Alberto's prize Brahmas and we were afraid they'd kill themselves. I wanted the drug which would have the least propensity to combine with whatever exotic plant they had eaten to become so wild. I couldn't quite explain my problem and finally asked to see the selection, since the man thought anything would do, and then read the labels. I chose one brand and asked for enough for ten calves.

The pharmacist went to the back of the store to get the drugs and I waited patiently. Another customer came in, a tall police colonel. The counters and shelves suddenly seemed too small, and the lack of windows confining. The colonel strutted about, a huge peacock in armor, wearing a black leather cyclist's jacket, a heavy black gun, a black-handled knife, a silver belt buckle. The boots clicked on the stony floor, and I felt he was stalking something by intimidation rather than stealth. He finally stopped and leaned on the counter ten feet away from me, and checked his moustache and angle of his military-style cap in the counter mirror.

He belonged in some movie and I tried to ignore him. The pharmacist came back with a case of tranquilizers and a box of hypodermic needles and he began to figure out the bill. I told him to charge it to the Abulafia Ranch, and then I signed for it. As soon as the transaction was completed, I was addressed by the colonel.

"Americano," he called.

"Señor?"

"You have your papers?"

"In my car, Señor."

"Very well, but I would like to see them." He followed me outside to the jeep and watched while I stored the package in the back and then unlocked the glove compartment. My papers were perfectly in order and I gave them to him and started the car while his aide joined him and looked them over also.

"This is a one-year working visa," he said, and I agreed.

"You are this person," he said.

"Those are my papers."

"You will have to come to the station, Señor."

"Por qué?" I exclaimed, not being at all sure what was bothering him, whether it was the drugs I had purchased, the fact that I was American, or that I lived at the Abulafia.

"You don't look like the picture on this visa," he said, "and yet this car goes with these papers."

Even looking at the picture upside down in his hands, I could tell that there would be no arguing with him. I was darker, leaner, and my hair much longer, since the time I had applied for the visa, and the car mirror revealed that even my features had changed. I felt it would be best if I explained at the station among other people. He said: "Write your name below this signature here."

I did.

"They don't match," he said.

"Of course they do," I said, looking again. "I just used a different kind of pen."

"Why do you insist you are this person?" he continued officiously.

"I think we can clear this up quickly."

"No, no," he said, "this will take some time. We must find out who you are and why you would buy these drugs."

"Anyone from the ranch will identify me, if you notify them that I am here."

"Someone from there may come into town after you, and then we would know."

"I am in a very big hurry to return with this medicine."

"Everyone is always in a hurry," he said casually.

"This could be a matter of life and death," I said, thinking how much the calves were worth.

"Both are common," his friend said.

"Why?" I stammed. "Why are you being so unreasonable?"

Both of them laughed and I felt ridiculous. "If this is a mistake," the colonel said, "we will find out later." He smiled.

They got in my jeep and we drove through the streets of the town with its pastel blue, green, and pink houses lining the hilltops until we came to an old adobe building, a remnant of another era, which should have been allowed to collapse like its small annex whose roof was a wreath of branches from crooked trees. That three-story main building served as both police station and jail. Inside, various attempts at remodeling had brought it into the twentieth century, so that everything around me had the taste of World War Two America, of U.S. surplus. My hope was that there would be enough efficiency here to get me out quickly. But I had shown weakness, and I realized that they would have their fun. I had been so preoccupied with returning to the ranch that I hadn't noticed that the colonel was testing me, and so had made the wrong countermove by pleading. I was angry, but reconciled myself to wait for something to free me.

They led me into a small corridor off the main lobby. It contained three small cells, and I was told to wait in one. There were no windows, and the corridor had simply been divided by sliding jail doors. My portion was six feet square and contained a single chair. There was one small door in the wall opposite me. I was resting with my eyes open, trying to pass the time by taking in all the details around me: examining cracks in the floor, carvings on the walls, and the shiny door rails set awkwardly into the slanting concrete.

I absently began playing with a few tinny Mexican coins from my pocket, tossing them up in the air to see if they would make heads fifty percent of the time. Might as well relax, I told myself, just as the main door opened and a guard, a meager man, entered, pushing before him a young Indian. I did not recognize what tribe he belonged to, but he was evidently quite drunk or quite sick. He didn't look at me as he passed by. The guard opened the last cell on the corridor, and just as the Indian entered, he began to cough, an awful retching sound. Methodically the guard closed the door. The Indian slumped into a corner and became still. The vomit smell permeated the small enclosed area instantly. The guard looked at me, then down at the Indian, and for some reason decided to be good-natured. He opened the door to the outside to let in some fresh air. I was already perspiring on this hot day, and the breeze barely relieved me. Outside I could hear hammering, preparations for the *Cinco de Mayo* celebration.

The Indian man did not respond to me or to the guard's leaving. I asked him what was wrong but he did not speak Spanish, or any dialect I knew. Because of the dam, there was a new law in effect—not an official one—that if an Indian was caught armed or wandering around in the mountains along the border, he was brought in for questioning, or worse. He would be released only if he could state his place of living or his employment.

This man had been caught, maybe beaten, and brought here for no reason that he could discern. He was a strong, broad-featured young man who despite his pain sat motionless and totally silent. Not even his eyes spoke, or acknowledged my presence. The smell of his own vomit was of no concern to him, and the blood from his cut feet mingled with it on the floor.

No one disturbed me or my wounded and intractable companion until it was about time to eat. There was more movement outside the corridor, and someone banging against the door shook my concentration, and I dropped one of the coins. It fell by the railing and I didn't bother to pick it up. But while I was waiting for what I hoped might be a glass of water, I kept looking at it, round and shiny and useless. I was having a hard time making do with nothing. The boredom was making me anxious. I wondered if the Indian with me was impassive or somewhere else.

There was no longer any light coming through the open

door. It was cooling off, and I had reached the point of not caring where I would sleep, of not caring about a glass of water or about someone's bringing me food. It was enough to be left sitting in the dark corridor while the fresh night breeze came in smelling of oranges. I laughed, seeing myself quite clearly from some distant vantage point, just sitting quietly in a cell as if it were a porch.

My last frivolous act before the door opened and the guard came in with a soup bowl was to shove the coin into the railing with the tip of my boot. I didn't say anything, maybe I was whistling or humming, or singing a tune from the radio. I just watched him while he tried to open the door after unlocking it: noticed how quickly it became stuck a foot along its track. The guard fought with it, put his weight against it, and this caused him to believe the trouble was along the top rail. He had to put my bowl down. Here, every job is fractured into several parts, each allotted to only one man. This man's job wasn't opening stuck doors, so he went to get help.

The coin had bent and wedged in the door so that it would not slide in any direction. How typical it was that the man took the keys from the lock connected to nothing! There was room for me to squeeze out the opening, just barely, but I was held back by the moans of my companion. His complaint came from across a great distance, from someplace between where he was and this corridor. I wanted to help him but didn't know how to at the moment. At least, there was someone who would come for me. Brito might take time off from working with Silvera on the new village, or he might send one of the hands, or a message to someone in town to inquire after me—all I had to do was wait.

And yet I was anxious to get going; it was night and there was no reason to trouble anybody. It was not my signature on the paper after all, and not my picture they had seen. It was best this way. I was no one, so how could they bother me again? Waiting for the guard to return with help, I felt that my time for decision was slipping away while I still had a chance to leave and the doors were open.

On the way home I could still picture a flock of Rurales searching the streets while I sat perched in the tangle of trees above the abandoned annex. It wasn't the fact that I was gone that bothered them, but that I'd had the audacity to try to escape, and yet they called off their search when their suppertime came. While the clouds crept across a blazing half-moon and the branches rustled their leaves in the wind, I finally came to see the meaning of Tsari's incantation—and that was really the beginning.

I was more in touch with myself, further along that mystery where in a moment we rediscover those strange flights of power. And it was they which served me that day when her time came.

Twenty-Three

"I feel free to make any connections that I can, for there seems to be a rhythm to them and then, an unfolding."

"It is a rhythm of little things; so when you fall you don't just get up and curse the ground. First you look around to see what the earth is trying to tell you."

"When I was on the verge of crossing over and was thinking about my fatherhood, I kept looking for some overall plan, to know if what I was doing was right."

"Sometimes we hear voices from the other side. They seem to come out of everything we see. They may mislead you, but the more familiar with them you become, the more you can trust them."

"I can never find them by looking. They come at times only to disappear and leave me talking to myself like a fool."

"*All I know is that when I see what is around me, there is also a course I must follow—like the river had to return to the canyon and my people had to return to the fields.*"

"*It is because you live in a spiritual world.*"

"*No, I have never seen a spiritual world.*"

"*You and I have different words for talking about what we know.*"

"*There is no difference. It is not a choice. We live here because this is our earth, and all around are its ways and the connections between them. It is just the way it is and there are always things to do.*"

"*When I began to believe you, I thought it would be harder to deal with life, yet I am not losing control, and sometimes there is power in my hands.*"

"*You have not lost your self as I once feared, but it is not the time to let others think you did anything unnatural. And since the birth was in me, it is only I who can say what happened. And when I speak I will remember that many fear what they do not understand.*"

Twenty-Four

For a week maybe, I hardly ate anything, for there was no more room inside me. The fruits of the prickly pear were in bloom, and because they were red and vermilion and soft with much juice, I ate as many as I could find. I would take them in my hand, thorns still fine and sharp on the oval pods, and squeeze them hard while it hurt and I tried to concentrate on what I had to do. Then I would lick the red juice which was sweet with good sugar from my hands. There was much kicking inside me when I did this, and I was saying that it was time to come out since there was no more room left.

Without warning there was a loud cry from my belly and I said, "Be still, for there is no room for loud cries." But the cry came again and since I was listening for it I could tell it was not the sound of a baby. The sound hurt and made me feel very weak. It was a sinking feeling and I knew this was not the sign of a birth but of a death. I tried not to know that Teresa had seen the center of the earth from this side for the last time. I tried not to listen but I went about the ranch afraid to look at the faces of the people who had come from the mountains, because one of them might have been the one to tell me it was true. I waited all day for someone to tell me and it was hard because I became so tense that there would be great seizures on my body, clamping down on the cry until I could no longer stand. When I lay down, it was hard then to get up as I felt much heavier. The ground seemed to hold me to it. I did not have to wait for someone to come tell me that things had changed and that I would not find her in the mountains again. I looked at their great shapes and saw only a huge stillness, like an antelope suspended in midjump. All the movement was now inside me, a pushing and a leaping about. I was so heavy that I was afraid and upset, wanting only to sleep and think. But they would not rest inside me; the cry had awakened them; perhaps they were too scared to stay quiet inside me. And just when I wished to rest, the two of them began to fuss and to want to come out.

She had touched my belly and been startled, and she had rubbed me with her hands and told me there would be two and not one. "It is a good sign," she said, "and it means that I can go and leave this place."

It was now all happening so quickly that I went to the

knoll in the arroyo where my arrows had entered, and did not want anyone to see me for my grief was very great. I was completely alone and the world was so small that I could hardly fit into it. I had to stop and kneel in the sand to catch my breath. It was uncomfortable everywhere until I reached the mesquite trees. Only there were my muscles and limbs free of the heaviness, and there I was able to hide myself, and found a soft spot where when I lay down it did not hurt.

Here, too, the children were still, and I was able to speak to the plants I brought with me and tell them what they must do. And when I said the things that Teresa had taught me, I became very sad, wanting again to see and speak to her. The knoll is a special place, and because it is in the middle, one can see to both sides. There were messages calling me to both at once, and I did not know where to turn. I was not sure about what to say to someone who was dying or to someone who was being born, and yet silence would not do. My frightened eyes would be an unwelcome slap in the face. Two moods tugged at me, and my feelings mixed like sand and water. It was hard to move in this mud, or to know what to say and do. She was so close to me that I wished to hold her and yet there was this fighting inside me which cried to be free of my own bonds.

I never thought I would find death and birth at the same place. The more I rested and relaxed the more I drifted toward Teresa. And still as I was not with my babies, they hurt me more, and the pains would sneak up on me. It was like this when J.P. came. I heard his voice and then I had to carry on two conversations.

"You should not have followed me," Teresa said when I saw her standing on the ledge.

"You should not have followed me," I said to J.P., for it is not good for a man to witness a birth. There are many things that can happen to a man; most of them are very bad, and only one is good. It would take a strong man who is ready. From the first I heard of his voice—and could hear the weakness—I was afraid for him. He looked at me and did not see me at all, and I had no idea where his concentration was.

"What are you doing here alone?" they both asked me at once, and I was much confused. Teresa was telling me to return to my babies, and J.P. wanted to stay. By now he should have known that one can be in more than one place at once, and I could hardly love him while he was so foolish.

I wanted him to leave, but with the same words that I spoke to him, I made Teresa go further from me, and I was not sure I could ever find her again.

"Are you gone?" I called out the minute I could not see her anymore, and just then my bag of water broke as if a hand had been thrust down my passageway. I was hit by another wave spiraling through my body and tried to hold it back, for I knew it could do no good since the two of them were locked together inside. The one on the bottom had its backside down, and the other's head was by its feet. So they could not come down until they turned. I wanted to save all my strength until they did, and not to stay with J.P. But he would not listen. He was trying to be kind when he should have been smart.

Teresa could not tell me what to do, for she had always taken the tall mint herb and even when she was young she hadn't allowed any babies to pass through her. The times were bad, with much fighting between Yaquis and Mexicans, and she did not want to have a child then. When she would not speak when I beseeched her, I felt that for sure I would die from the struggling inside me. Or that J.P. would have to take my death from me and go himself. This would not have been fair, for it was not his fault. It was the will of those two inside me who did not want to face the world when they no longer had a home, and who were frightened by the cry of someone going the other way through the great *muhs*. I could look in and clearly see the twins embraced together, sideways in my womb. It was too hard for them to turn as long as Teresa was still in the passageway. I was not ready for her to go, not ready for them to come.

Then, the thing happened which surprised and delighted me because I thought I might have done something wrong by letting a white man inside me, and that all the troubles that had come to the village were because I had not listened to my chief. J.P. now might have thought I was sleeping, but he took his hands and put them to my belly, and as far away as I was, I felt they were different. There was a heat of concentration, just as there had always been in Teresa's touch. And though he pressed firmly on me, I could not feel the weight of his body, only his hands which were truly feeling and went from one place to another as if they knew what they were doing. I don't know if I smiled with my face, yet I felt a wonderful warmth because his touch could be so soothing.

He had learned to hold his breath inside him so it would not interfere, and he had gone round and round inside himself so that the heat had come, and the force had reached the surface of his fingers. I didn't think he would ever do it. He was touching me with his eyes. I dared not speak because it would disturb him and he was about to find out what he should have known for a long time. Perhaps he had taken some of the mushroom, but I did not know because I had not been watching him. Slowly, as if by some painful effort, I felt his eyes entering the passageway, and looking inside with my own.

His fingers found the small head and moved down along the arm to the legs and then to the feet. Then they traced the outline of the other one's head, and then its chest and stomach, until he finally touched the other's feet. He found out that the bottom one's backside was down into the passage, and that it could not pass. I expected that at this point he would panic and cry out, that he would waste all his strength. Brito had always said that a man who could find water would have some powers to reach where normal eyes could not see. It was delight to have him looking with me. He began rubbing my belly in a circular fashion, but there was as yet no will in his motions. They were helpful only because they went the right way. He could not have known which way the twins had to turn unless he was seeing into the passageway, unless he finally saw how it was on the other side and where it was possible to move, and where it was obstructed.

"Harder," I said. But he only pushed down on me and it hurt more. The pain frightened me, then I began looking for Teresa again.

Twenty-Five

Because I was on the knoll, it was easy to travel, and it was easy to look this way and that way.

"You should not make me laugh because it hurts," I told the small dog I came across in the woods. It was the same dog I had played with as a child and now he would not listen to me, but continued to chase his shadow around a large tree trunk until he would trip on his hind legs and fall, and roll over. "Do you think I have time to play with you now?" I asked but the dog paid no attention and would not even answer to his name. I thought he would follow me as I walked home but he didn't come after me. Soon I saw some wild turkeys which I had not seen for a long time. I found a good throwing stick and began to chase them through the woods. I wanted to kill one of the big males so that I could look at it and ask it what kind of man I would have when I grew up. My mother said that only a turkey cock would know.

For a little while, the turkeys and I went around and around in the trees, but they kept the branches between us and leapt from the stick as if forewarned. I soon grew tired and decided to return to the village before it got dark. The trees hid my way but I sought out the sound of the river flowing through the barranca and kept following it, keeping the splashing flow to my left.

I tried running and then walking, but it was not like either, a movement of flowing down the steep path of the mountain as if caught in a downdraft. The trail led to the village and I had been on it a thousand times. So I listened for the sound of people, and looked for the light of the fires. But it was now very still and pitch dark.

Because it was so dark I stumbled among the trees and shrubs, my feet catching in the tangle of grasses as if they were trying to trip me. I should have slowed down, but could not. I began running. Somehow I was going uphill and the higher I got the closer I came to a moaning sound that was so human I thought someone was in trouble. I began drifting toward the sound. Everything moved as I passed except the old wolf. This one was a big gray whose skin had turned to bones, who sat on his haunches, still as fire, and stared across a field of barren rock.

When he saw me he let out a frightful howl and began circling on his spot. I heard that note of despair curdled into

the painful cry and listened carefully as it echoed unan-
swered. I wanted to weep because there was no mate to answer him; he was a lone survivor whose voice carried alone
through the whole mountain range. But he said, "What do
you want?"

"I am looking for Teresa."

Again he howled and pointed his snout to the sky and a
moon appeared, a great orange moon. "Have you seen her?"
I asked.

"Have you tried the village?"

"I can't find it," I said.

"Then you must keep going, it is very easy to pass things
by. Do you know how to tell the living from the dead?"

"The last time I saw her she was on the ledge of the canyon. If I do not find her I will die."

"That is no matter, so go to the village first and if she
is not there, then go to her hut, but leave me now, for you
are interrupting the silence and I must concentrate on what
I must become."

I tried very hard to get back into the downdraft and to
follow the trail by insight, following the memory glyphs, and
kept falling through a coil where the images turned into
feelings, and the feelings into places, and finally I reached
a spot I knew, where my mother had had me and which
only she and I knew. It was where my afterbirth was buried.
From here I was able to find the path to the village. Suddenly, I was in the middle of it. I looked around and only
smelled ashes. The fire had taken away all the corrals and

all the roofs, and only the adobe walls were left where once all our houses stood. I looked for the great cloud in the sky but there was only a gray smoke above me. It would never be the same again, and my children would never see what I had loved and the way it was when my mother lived here. Because the flow was broken I was sad. There was no place for my children to live and I thought of them working in the mine. It made me afraid and then the village was alive with beings who were afraid because I had had such thoughts in their midst and had disturbed their contemplation on what they were to become. They chased me away with their bad winds and I went to where Teresa had always lived.

Around her hut it was very bright; a fire seemed to be burning around it. The hut stood in the middle and I went inside to see if she was there. All her medicine bundles were gone and I wondered where she had taken them, for I wished to have them. I looked outside and a little girl was standing in front of the fire. She was crying and tearing at a dress which was the same one I remembered wearing at her age. I told her to stop or she would ruin it, but this only made her scream and fall to the ground and kick. There was nothing I could say that would make her stop. We just looked at each other for a long time while we both cried, and waited in the light of Teresa's hut.

When she did not return I went back inside and much to my surprise I noticed a big hole in the center of the floor. I was sure it had not been there before. Then I was sure Teresa had fallen in. Looking down it made me dizzy and before I could help myself I was inside this black hole. But I did not fall. I was floating as if on my back on a wave in the ocean. It was a comfortable feeling and I did not care if I ever went anywhere else again.

Twenty-Six

There was a voice calling to me which I could not recognize. The voice had a firm command to it, was gentle and yet penetrating with a nice pleasant melody to it. I decided to listen and hear what it was saying and at first I could not understand too well because there was a lot of hard breathing in between the words. And it kept fading in and out. Because I could not hear well, I thought there was something seriously wrong with me. It was something about hands and arrows. I did not feel any pain or any movement but when I tried to sit up my legs were being held tightly around the ankles.

"Use my hands to pull yourself up, I have something to tell you."

"What is it?" The voice was J.P.'s, only it did not sound like him. His words were calm, his voice mellow.

"I have found your arrows."

"What arrows?"

"Do you know where you are?"

"Yes."

"Do you know what you have been doing?"

"I have been resting."

"You have been thrashing around like a madwoman. I thought you were going to kill yourself or the babies."

"I'm all right now. What is this about arrows?"

"Not long ago, I thought I heard a wolf howling. I've never heard a wolf so I wasn't sure. But then I went outside and knew it wasn't a coyote or a dog. When I looked down, a wind from the arroyo blew sand in my eyes and the moonlight shone on your arrows. I told you they would be here; they were buried in the sand."

"Why are you telling me this?"

"Because I know what is wrong."

"What?" I barely believed he was there.

"You have, I mean, you are going to have twins. That's why you are so big and why your labor has begun so early."

"I know that."

"Then you don't mind if I help you? You will have another contraction in just a few minutes."

"Why am I so bloody?"

"I think it's natural. The last barrier has broken. I don't know why they won't turn. I'm sure the one on the bottom is supposed to turn so that its feet or head will come out."

"I'm glad to be talking with you again," I said.

"We don't have much time, Tsari. Do you know what to do?"

"I don't think I can talk any more, but I am glad you found the arrows. Perhaps they will help."

"Don't relax."

J.P. kept telling me not to relax and for that reason I did not lie down. I sat with my back propped against a mesquite tree and watched my belly. It did not make sense that the baby would not turn. But it was not my baby anymore. It was his and he had always been stubborn. If it did not come out, it was actually his fault, and so I watched him to see what he would do. When I started to tighten up in pain, he yelled at me to breathe hard. I couldn't pay attention to both him and the contraction, and because of his voice, he was the stronger. I kept watching him and he was so funny showing me how to take in a deep breath that I was barely able to do it without laughing, or crying. We kept huffing and puffing so long that I thought he was going crazy doing all those antics in front of me. It was not like him at all to be so silly. He never let loose like that. It would be nice if he were able to play like this more often. I was thinking about this when the pain began to pass away. I reached the green thorns of the mesquite and broke a twig off, for it would be dangerous to leave the babies again and I could use the thorns to keep awake. I knew that the pushing would start by morning and that if the babies did not turn by then, I would burst. "You have to turn the baby," I said. "It is your baby on the bottom. It is as simple as that."

J.P. took off his shirt and began fiddling in the sand using one of the arrows. I wondered how he knew to do this. Just watching him relax this way made me feel more hopeful, and I cleaned some sweat and blood off me with the sand. My dress was no good and I ripped it off by shredding it, and he didn't look at me at all while I did these things. It was not my body that the moon struck, for it was pale with a bluish tinge, and swollen all over like a fat Mexican. I was glad he wasn't looking. I felt he would never want to "make love" as he called it with me again for fear that I would change like this again.

When the wave came over me the next time, I caught it at the beginning and began breathing and trying to think only about him. He didn't have to hold me down, but he had to keep rubbing my legs to keep the muscles from cramping. I could not clench my fist because of the thorns I held. I breathed so much to get over the wave that I became dizzy before I could breathe out again. I was weak and nauseous, barely able to keep sitting up.

I could feel that J.P. was again rubbing my stomach with his hands, not pushing or shoving at the babies but massaging them with all the strength in his fingers. I closed my eyes and soon it felt as if he were sucking at my nipples for they felt much cooler. I drew my legs up as if to receive him and had no idea why this was what I felt like doing. I had never heard him singing but now he was singing in the chanting voice as he rubbed his hands around and around on my belly, going lower and lower and suddenly I was not sure whether his hands were on the inside or the outside of me. The singing made no sense and sounded like English, but it did not matter because he was forcing a movement inside me. It felt like he was making love to me, and yet his desire was much stronger than I had ever felt it before. His massages brought on another contraction, and I waited for it to start hurting but my feelings were so confused that the wave felt warm and only brushed against me, making me feel bathed and washed, and I remember tasting salt in my mouth.

My belly began to tingle, like that feeling that comes when a limb goes to sleep, and I felt as if I had just swallowed a great gulp of water and it was rushing down and sloshing around in the belly. The hands were washing in this water although I could not feel them touching me anywhere.

He said: "You are the lust of birth I am the great creator You descend to the place of birth I am the great bringer-out Six hours we are ready for you to move Six hours we have waited for you to turn Turn by means of your mother Turn by means of your father I seized you I am your mother I am your father You are the white snake You are the red snake Turn again vigorously as I pluck you out."

He did not believe in charms, he did not know incantations, and yet because of his children locked inside me, he made, or tried to remember, old words. I could feel the truth of them and the force of his intentions, just as my sister had finally heard me in the darkness of her youth. It brought on another contraction, this one much stronger than all of the others so that I had to howl and could not even breathe in or out, and yet the scream getting out of me was powerful, and it caught the babies inside it so that they were thrust about and moved around. The scream froze him, but the babies were rearranged and made to sit straight inside. I was glad to let such a great scream go forth, one which had been held inside for so long and which needed to be expelled with a great upheaval of the bowels. It drove the sleeping birds from the. trees, and it drove the heaviness from off my heart and chest. It must have gone a long way, far enough to let the old women know what I was doing, for as the scream disappeared over the hills, the reed flute began playing.

Twenty-Seven

At that time there was no time to rest, no time to talk, and only moments to get ready for the next wave that would hold me in its onrush. The waves were strong and would not let me think about anything else, and keeping up with the breathing was also hard. It would not hurt if I could keep the strings in my body loose, yet sometimes I was twisted by the wave and this pulled me in many ways at once. My back was sore from rubbing up against the rough bark, but the tree gave me support and I would not move away. When it calmed, I would watch the way the limbs of the trees would weave together in the breeze and interrupt the stars, and then knot them together again. The night was lovely and warm and the wind itself seemed to circle the knoll on its path through the arroyo. The bare earth and sand kept my heat and was the blanket to my nakedness. And in these calms the notes of the flute would be long and soft so that I could be soothed. Then, as the wind and the leaves moved, and as the reed fluttered, I prepared for the next one and could keep tune breathing with the changing notes that got to such a high pitch before dropping down gradually to the long low notes. I just obeyed. I had no choice and I was thankful for the playing. I knew I had chosen the right spot.

Soon came the signals to start pushing, and it was very uncomfortable to have my legs out, to have my backside on the ground. But those waves, a little less powerful now, kept me off balance so I was afraid to get up. He was doing well until this time when everything began happening at once, and now the confusion in his eyes was not pleasing. I sent him to get some water and told him where I had hidden the bowl. It would have been best if he didn't have to return, for he had seen enough, all that a man should see if he does not want to become a mixed soul. Most men know this and stay away but if he would stay until the end and be again caught by the cord, well, I would have him, for another pair of hands would be useful with two babies being born.

I had never known or heard of a woman who had to do two at once. Teresa, who was so old that she could not count the years, and had helped many women after their babies came, had never seen two at once. The Indians never had this happen to them around here, and yet we knew that it had happened. I knew the story of the woman who had the two at once in a time when there were many more tribes living in the mountains. The people were afraid of her, and her own people would hardly go near her children. They grew up alone and were not allowed to have relatives. She stayed with her people but the children were not taught the ways and the male child did not belong. It is said that they grew up and mated with each other alone in the woods. They did not join any tribe but kept to themselves and wandered. It was a race apart and many people called the descendants of these children witches and other horrible names. They always lived alone and were feared, but now there were none of these people left.

I had made up my mind to have the two at once. I would do it. I was not going to be afraid. If the story were true then it was meant to be. It took a stranger to make it happen again, and he was not an unkind man.

My mother had pushed me out with great speed and I would do the same. I felt light and strong when I got up and squatted down with my feet planted firmly in the loose earth. I am a strong woman and when it came time to push I did it without having to labor or to strain myself. I liked this position and liked the feeling of pushing. But I had to pant almost like a dog, and to blow out hard to keep upright. When the goats had their babies, at this time they would always be turning around and looking at us like they did not know what was happening. They always looked so funny when they bleated while pushing that I was glad not to see myself. When I heard J.P. coming back with the water I wished there was a way to keep him out.

The passageway was so full that I could not stop or speak, or straighten up. I knew he was there but I could not really see him. For once he went about his business without bothering to try and help. He was making soap suds from the yucca in the bowl while I reached my fingers where I could feel the baby's head. And with my own fingers I could tell when to push and when to make the opening rounder. The reed flute was playing a familiar song and while I was listening to it, this part became very easy to do.

Then, with one great push the boy child came out, and I guided him along my arm with his tiny wet face cupped in the palm of my hand. He was bathed in my white fluids but already had motions of his own. The face was old but I had seen one like it before. It was hardly mine from the start, and must have come from a place far from here for it was very thin and long. I knew right away that he would have a beard. I knelt down and held him against my stomach with the pale white cord hanging along my thigh. Right away I scraped away the coating from his nose and mouth. Then I gave him to J.P. to hold. The boy wiggled and almost squirmed out of his hands but he was not clumsy with it and took it as if it were any baby animal.

"It is beautiful," he said. "It has eyes like an owl. I will listen to see how well it breathes."

His hands were again with power and worked independent of the doubt expressed by his face, and with a strength that was greater than his tired eyes. He asked me if I was all right and I told him it was he who had changed, but I could not speak much of it. From my dress I pulled the thick threads and began to bind them around the cord. I wound them very tight. I told him to close his eyes and hold the baby very tight. Then as the cord stopped pulsing I did what was necessary so that the other might come down without getting entangled. When I saw that the blood smell was making him weaker I asked him to take the baby to the bowl and wash it. The night was filled with its screaming but I had no time to worry.

Already I was being washed clean by the breaking of the second bag of waters which eased the burning sensation of my bottom lips. I was ready for the girl to come out and greet me. Her brother's screaming had drowned out the sound of the flute, or maybe it had stopped since I would be able to do it alone this time. In the moments I had to rest I made a private prayer to those who had helped me.

It was a long time waiting and it was beginning to be light when I had to start pushing again. He kept telling me that this one had a longer way to go and he had to hold me from behind because I was becoming tired and because this child did not seem to be able to make up her mind. I was not able to do anything to help but had to obey all the laws of my body at this time. Somehow I bit my lip and this cut let blood run down over my breasts, and I could taste it in my throat. He gave me a piece from inside of the barrel cactus and this wetness and nourishment began to help me. I tried breathing and relaxing but the pain came because I was too tired to keep up.

When the girl's feet reached the entrance I would have gladly torn her body loose from me. But he did a smart thing at this time. He gave me the boy to put to my breast, and with his hands he began to ease the little body between the bone and the passageway. The suckling child made me forget about pushing hard, and I let him do the taking of it. The boy bit at my nipple as I tried to help him drink. He was so small that I wondered if he could survive. Yet J.P. was right: those eyes had let me know that he would. Right from the start he scratched and bit me.

"Open more," he said, and when I tried to I fell down on my backside. The girl child was born with me resting my legs on his shoulders and exposing my innermost parts to him. When his hands became so gentle they worked as if they were my own; I knew that I would have power with him because he did this. It would not be so much back and forth laughing as before, but the one good thing had happened: he had found the power of the hands, and he could touch with his eyes, so that he too could heal. I knew that he had a power I would never have, so that we would have to be two partners and could not easily leave each other.

The head was finally at the entrance and though I had a great urge to push, he knew of it at the same instant, and warned me without speaking that I had to suppress it. I arched my back and moaned, O and O and O, and I did not let the push come, though my eyes were straining as I held it and the tears came.

I fell back sobbing and through the tears beheld what

beautiful black hair the girl child had, and how long and straight it was. The boy was in the crook of my arm, still tugging at the breast that fell to the side. The girl child was bigger and rounder and with the cord stretching I hugged her to me, rubbing her clean with my hair and then pinching her so that she would take her breath without me.

Gradually as the light came in and I could see my own hair below the navel, this one's cord stopped throbbing and became loose and pale. I had all my breath back and could take in great chestfuls of air with my lungs free. But he was tired, and he lay still with his face against my thigh. The bowl was near me and I stretched for it and brought it to my side and began washing the girl and letting the soap flow between my legs and cool me as it dried. The little one tried to smile even when she cried and she had my eyes, very wide eyes, that knew me.

And still it was not over. After just a short time I had another contraction. It woke him and because I complained he had to start the massaging of my belly again while I held both the babies to my breasts.

"Is it whole for you now?" I asked him.

"As if you and I are no longer separate people."

"You belong to this tree now, do you know that? You belong to these babies even if they are not ours. You belong to me even though I am only half yours."

"This search to find each other . . . I think it's always going to happen again."

"Yes, but it is different now. Our love is an agreement

like the one Teresa had with the powers so that she could live just so long and not a moment longer."

"At least I don't feel there is anything to be afraid of anymore."

"Only the afterbirth. It must come out and soon. If I am not to bleed to death, I have to make a mixture of the *gomilla*. It was Teresa's last gift so that I would not hemorrhage and die after having two at once. It is a wonder that she knew so much. I feel the contraction coming on; push harder."

"Breathe deep," he said, as it began again.

Twenty-Eight

The rest was easy, only it should have been over, for after so long they were outside me. After so long they had their own voice. But I still had to expel the little sac that had nourished them, and then when it was out and I rested a short while, I had to prepare the *gomilla* and let the powder dissolve in water until it became a brown-yellow. I was good and thirsty and drank the bowl twice, knowing that the plant would stop the bleeding and allow me to go on. There was still much to do because there were still laws to follow which were just like the ones my body followed in the delivery.

It was first the custom to bury the placenta in the same spot where the baby was born, and though there were two babies there was only one placenta I could see and it would have to serve as the marker of the spot where they both entered this side. I hoped they had both thought well and carefully on what they were to be before they left the other. There are laws on that side also, and I hoped they'd had the time to have learned what was to be done so that they would not waste their strength in fighting against themselves and in thinking thoughts which would be of no use. I should have been overjoyed and happy but it was not all so, since I had been to the other side and had been with Teresa and knew it would not be easy for these two, and felt how unnatural it would be if they had their own children and how it would be when people looked at them. They already said strange things about Teresa and me, and my uncle was no help to us. Yet when they didn't understand the laws or why one thing happened after another, they would come to me. I knew this. I knew they would come to the two babies in their turn.

What would everyone think when a gringo was with me? Even other whites did not believe that a gringo could do anything special. We Indians have always felt the desert belongs to us alone with all its secrets, but this was no longer so with J.P. here.

Now, he was not too sure what it was all about. I think he would have left the shelter as it was, and not put the afterbirth down so deep. But I took pains to make the ground just like it was before I came, like even a cat would, and to make sure that nothing could enter this place and steal the power which was ours. I mean that after a birth there lingers about all the strength which has gone into crossing over. It must not be robbed or there will be no getting back. If there were no returning, this life would be a prison indeed, and there would be no other chances to think it out again. We say: "Among us they come, among us they go. New are their garments, new are their ways. They shall not die out. Let the sorcerers guard the crossing between the here and the hereafter."

"What are you thinking about?" he asked me when I finally sat down to rest and to hold my babies.

"I do not feel fresh yet," I said. "I would very much like to wash myself, and to let the sun come down and shine on clean skin."

"We are finished here. I would like to show everyone what the babies look like, and then I want something to eat."

"Would you pass off what has happened for us so quickly? Just eat and go on again as if it were yesterday? There is plenty of time here for a big event." I knew very well that he would want to go to the ranch but I didn't want him to forget what he had seen until it had become a firm part of him. This would take time; and there was another reason. "I will go to wash now while the morning is still fresh."

"It has been a long night and our children are very beautiful."

"Only to us," I said. "To others they will be frightening."

"Just because they are twins?"

"No, but because of what is said about twins."

"I am not superstitious and neither is Brito, so I would not worry about this."

"You do not know how hard it is to return to a place after you have changed," I told him, and asked that he be patient. "If you could only see yourself," I laughed, "then you would not be so quick to go back." If I did not think he was a good man to have around, I would have been scared of him. When people go loco and run around in the woods for some time they begin to look like he looked, hair tangled in strands, dried blood on his skin, pollen on his beard, lines creasing the face, and rabid eyes, swollen for lack of sleep and yet staring at everything at once.

And still it was he who had been caring most for the babies, because I had to make a small fire and get ashes to rub on the navel cord, and to walk around so that my belly would get firm again. So he held them after we were at the place in the arroyo where it narrowed and went deep. There were flat rocks, one under the other, and clear running water passed over them, catching at the basin at the lowest part. I will always remember that it was one of those clear still days when there are sheer white clouds in the sky which don't pass by but seem to rise up higher and higher until we can't see them anymore. It was a perfect day, I think.

I sat on the warm rocks. He let the babies sleep on his hairy stomach. The water became cloudy as I mixed it and rinsed it over my body. The sun warmed the water on my body and then left a cooling feeling as it dried. There was enough yucca soap left to wash my hair and this felt best of all. But when I was all clean I felt too naked without any clothes at all, and my bottom lips were swollen and stuck out beyond my hair. It hurt even to touch them. I took J.P.'s shirt and made that do the best I could. It was long and covered most of me. When all this was through, I picked up each baby and examined it closely to see if both had all their parts and were healthy. They were both so light and small that touching them did not feel at all like holding another human being.

It was strange to watch them trying to use their legs as if by stretching them out they could move. And I began to wish it were possible for them to just move anywhere without having to learn to put one foot in front of the other as if they were merely hobbled horses. It was told that there were once wise men with great powers in this region, and that they could move about by jumping and could cover great distances in no time at all. It would be a useful thing to know in the mountains where there were few roads. I supposed that this old story was true and wished I had the knowledge of how to teach legs to be this way. It would certainly make the way we lived a lot easier.

I wished Teresa could have been with me, and that she would have remained long enough to teach my babies all that she could do with her hands. At the beginning they would know, as they reached out and grasped the air, that there were real forces which felt only like air in one way, but which in another way could be held firmly. Their hands could make things live or die, could heal, and could make all live things grow and flourish. I knew so much of the voice that Teresa had taught me that I was afraid the knowledge of her hands would be lost with me, but now my children might learn it from their father.

The girl child was made for just this place where I had grown up; her tiny form revealed how she would grow and I could tell that having babies would be easy for her. But the boy was meant for another place. His chest and lungs were small, and not very good for climbing and running in the mountains. I had also, when very young, seen a man with his kind of face, and this man lived in one of the isolated valleys where few went because they were so hard to get into, and where it was easy to live.

I thought about this place deep in the Sierra Madre and felt that the boy should grow up like it was there and one day leave with his sister who might be his wife. I was sure they would go to a new country, but I was not sure of the place exactly or what the people were like there, and yet I knew that like this boy they would be different without being only Indian, Mexican or White.

As for now, I cuddled them both to me, and with much love kissed them both while they were mine. While they cried. And in their unformed voices I heard the sounds I would teach them to use so that they could speak to the plants and animals and call the birds, for often in these mountains it is lonely and there are no other people around to speak with.

"Where should we go?" J.P. asked me.

I had not given much thought to where I would go, but now that I felt somewhat drained, I wanted to go where I could rest easily and regain all my strength. "Brito's garden would be the best place," I said. The moment I made this choice my mood became calmer and I began thinking about the plants I had tended.

"It's a long way from here walking, but Tamayo's cabin at the back of the canyon would be fine."

I began to agree with him but I had an odd feeling that we were really close to the place. "It's not so far," I said.

"It will take us the whole afternoon to get there."

"No," I said, "it will take an hour." I could feel that it would not take longer, although I knew it would be many miles by the road. I knew then that I was standing at the center of the world and that all my senses were with me. I could feel where I was and where my plants were. I could not believe I had always walked so far to get such a short distance. This sense of being close came first and then I imagined how it could be. "We are at the tail of the S the arroyo makes," I said, "and the garden is at the head. We go straight across and enter the garden from the back. We don't have to use the road."

He got up and went to a spot at the edge of the arroyo and began to look over the hills. It took a few moments for him to locate himself. Then by turning around and around, he was able to judge just where every place was. Soon he came back and said, "You are right, but it seems impossible that we could be so close."

"So," I said, "even the hills agree." I was laughing then, because birthing the babies was what finally made it possible for me to see without going to the top of a hill. I handed him a baby to carry as I only had two hands. I gave him the boy and as he had been through it with me, he, too, could appreciate him and treat him as a special person because he had seen into the other side where his intuitions about such things were sure. This was so, for it was our morning and we were leaving and there would be no more doubts.

"What did you say?" he asked, when hearing that I was talking to myself.

There were many thoughts on my mind for this was a place I would not forget, and yet it was best not to dwell here too long. I told him we were leaving our first house, and I had to smile, for it is said: "The first house is the house of gloom and inside there is only darkness."

This book was set in Electra, a typeface designed by W(illiam) A(ddison) Dwiggins for the Mergenthaler Linotype Company and first made available in 1935. Electra cannot be classified as either "modern" or "old-style." It is not based on any historical model, and hence does not echo any particular period or style of type design. It avoids the extreme contrast between thick and thin elements that marks most modern faces, and is without eccentricities that catch the eye and interfere with reading. In general, Electra is a simple, readable typeface that attempts to give a feeling of fluidity, power, and speed.

W. A. Dwiggins (1880–1956) began an association with the Mergenthaler Linotype Company in 1929 and over the next twenty-seven years designed a number of book types, the most interesting of which are the Metro series, Electra, Caledonia, Eldorado, and Falcon. In 1930 Dwiggins became interested in marionettes, and through the years he made many important contributions to the art of puppetry and the design of marionettes.

The book was composed, printed, and bound by American Book-Stratford Press, Inc., New York, N.Y. The typography and binding design are by Cynthia Krupat.